7 Erotica Sex Stories Of Threesomes

Hot Explicit Tales Of Romance, BDSM, Kink, and Sex For Women

Tracy Queen

Copyright© 2018 by Tracy Queen

All Rights Reserved, including the right to reproduce this book or portions thereof in any form whatsoever. This book is a work of fiction. Any references to historical events, real people, or real places are used fictiously.

Disclamer

This book is complete make belief. Any resemblance or similarity to real life events or per-sons is complete coincidental. The author does not promote the actions and sexual practice explo-red in this book… He nearly reports them.

Table of Contents

BLOWIN' OUT THE CANDLES 5

CARIBBEAN GET AWAY 37

FRANK'S WILD YEARS 49

DREAMS OF CALIFORNICATION 70

WORKIN' 9 TO 5, WHAT A WAY TO MAKE A LIVIN' 80

STAYS IN MEXICO.. 97

THE BIG PAYBACK.. 105

BLOWIN' OUT THE CANDLES

That particular Saturday, was going to be the sort of day that would leave a rather distinct mark on my life; to say that it basically hogtied, whipped and kicked out the window my old sexual forays would be to sell short the whole lasting imprint. The day was going to turn out to be a madcap calvacade of filth, hijinks, bare-naked circus acts and more gooey bits than at a dentist office.

My name is Nick, just Nick… wouldn't want you to scour the net or local Yellow Pages to get a fix or GPS waypoint to tract me down. For the rest of this tale just call me Nick. Think of it like Witness Protection, only instead of Narcos, Mobsters and sketchy Russian Oligarchs, I'm setting up shop in the moorlands, hunkering down like a survivalist and leaving outside the grid, on account of pestering perverts.

Anyway, the day was off to a smashing start. The pillars of a great, fantastic and possibly idyllic Saturday were being ticked off some cosmic checklist. The birds were doing their interpretation of Vivaldi's Seasons; the Sun was baking everything into a tanned stupor; the wind was giving the warm weather a good fight; heat wave and wind chill were exchanging bad glances over a table and realizing they were at a stalemate. Everything was just Goldilocks perfect.

A freshly brewed cup of Java sat like a chalice on my hand and waves of caffeine meth were worming their way into my nostril. The quaint little day might as well have been a morning cartoon; all it needed was the Warner Brothers emblem and a cute little pig telling the audience to piss off. It was so on the nose perfect, that it might as well have a crosshair pointed pointed straight at its balls; the day was positively asking for some knave to come up next to it and punch its shit eating grin right off its smackers. It was inviting doom and desolation.

A banshee stubbed its toes and a wail started to gang-rape my idilic morning. The door bell went apeshit crazy. It rang once, twice, a third time and finally just got stuck. There I was, in my slippers, a cup of joe in my hand, in the middle of an air raid.

"Godammit," bliss went not only the way of the dodo but was taken out back and shot between the eyes, "fucking piece of shit."

"Man, it's Andy," a voice said outside my front door, "how the hell do I turn it off?"

"Andy, you prick, I told you a million times that asshole is wonky. Call me or text and I'll let you in, just don't ring the doorbell."

The thing keep up its fire alarm act. Upstair, the neighbors started stumping on the floor.

"Andy, bang it a little. Just bang it around the edges. Maybe it will get unstuck."

"I'm banging."

"Then kick it!"

"I'm kicking!"

"Put your elbow to it!"

"I'm putting my wrestling moves to it, the fucker won't quit."

"Just give me a second. Let me grab something."

I ran snatched my trusty doorbell fixer and hightailed it to door.

"Hey, man," went Andy as I swung open frame, "Jesus!" He flung back. "Overkill!"

Boom, bang, crack and a couple of more sounds mingled with the crazy bell as a brought my hammer down and did a Thor of the stupid thing.

"Andy," whack, "you," whack, "better," whack, "have," whack, "a good reason for fucking up my morning," whack, whack, whack, whack.

"I think you killed it. I think its ancestors actually felt it."

"What the hell do you want?" Andy and I had been closed friends; thick as thieves. We had hooked up in middle school, constant compadres. We were a Blake Shelton song.

"Two kindred spirits, bound by destiny. Well, now I was smart but I lacked ambition, he was wild an no inhibition…"

Our friendship was like mixin' fire with gasoline.

"You got a moment?" Went the desperado waiting for the Federales to catch up. "I need to talk to you 'bout somethin'."

"Come on in Andy," I handed him my cup of coffee. "I'll fix myself another one."

"Hazelnut creamer?"

"This is not a freaking Starbucks… You're lucky I didn't spit in it."

"You really aren't a morning person."

I flicked him the finger just to let him know that he'd hit the bullseye.

We sat on the couch and started running our gums off. We went to the whole male spectrum of chit chat. The Cubs. Dames in the bar. The government. Taco Bell's new enchilada. The whole bullshit sideway skip and leapfrog dance. Avoiding the issue like it was the plague.

"Andy, man, come out and say it… How much do you need this time?"

"What?" He peaked up.

"You're pussyfooting around the issue. Acting all scare… So what's the sum? How much do you need to borrow? I'll just put it on your tab."

"Geez, give the brother some credit."

"The brother? You're more albino than Casper. Andy, I have shit to do, so spill… How much dough do you need?"

"None, zip, zero," he put up his hands, "It's not that. It's not a cashflow problem. I'm not such a screwup… I just want you to fuck Penny."

Dead silence. You could, pardon the pun, have heard a penny drop. I stared at Andy. I stared at my cup of coffee. I stared at the rug. I stared back at Andy. I stared a second time at my cup of coffee. The rug? Wasn't giving up its secrets. Yup, I just had an aneurism.

"It stays between us. Just you and me," coughed Andy.

"What stays between us?"

"What I just said…"

"Andy, I'm pretty sure I just had a brain fart. You just told me you wanted me to fuck Penny."

"Yeah," like he had just asked me for a coin, pardon the pun once more, a penny, to put in the 7-11 jar, "fuck Penny. I want you to fuck Penny. Penny wants you to fuck Penny. Next Tuesday? We have her parents on the weekend; hitting the road on Friday. On Monday you and me are going out with the guys… They tell you which bar by the way? And on Thursday I got tickets to the new Marvel movie. So it has to be Tuesday. Or possibly Wednesday? Tuesday or Wednesday? Which day do you want to fuck Penny?"

"I'm I on candid camera? In that stupid Ashton Kutcher show? Is some asshole going to put out and YouTube this?"

"Are you stoned?" Andy asked.

"I'm I stoned? Andy, you git, you just asked me to fuck your wife. The same Penny that you have been dating since High School. The same Penny you took to the Prom. The same Penny you lost you V-Card to…"

"That was mutual."

"Right, right… The same Penny you moved in with 3 years ago. The same Penny you married last year."

"Yeah, Penny, you know her."

"Of course I know her, you dildo, we've been friends for over 12 years."

"So, will you fuck her?"

"Back the crazy train up and let's start from the get go," I stood up and started for the kitchen.

"Where are you going?" Went Andy.

"I need to Irish this up," I pointed at my cup. "You go on, I can hear you from the cupboards."

"So, you know we have been together for quite some time now."

"You're practically joined at the hips."

"We've been joking and trying to spice it up. She wasn't only my first, she was my only one."

"What about Karol?"

"A handjob in the woods isn't the same."

"You told me it was a blowjob," I grabbed the Wild Turkey and splash it in.

"Well, her mouth was close and some spittle got in the way. It was a blowjob by osmosis."

"3 years you cashed in that story. 3 freaking years it was 'blowjob this' and 'blowjob that'."

"Handjob, blowjob, same freaking thing."

"Only a celibate or man in a stable 12 year relationship can actually say that with an honest face."

"Let's get past the handjob. We're too hung up on the handjob."

"'Blowjob by osmosis'."

"Focus, Nick, my marriage is on the line."

"Something is defiantly on the line."

"Anyway, Penny and I, we've been talking… and last night it got serious."

"Go on…"

"We want a threesome. She asked me if we ever decided to have a threesome who would I want to join us. I wasn't sure if she was for real or not but I decided to take my chances and said Amanda, her hot blond friend from work."

"I've meet Amanda, and buddy you picked a winner. Legs up to her neck and to pair of knockers that could end world hunger."

"A yoga teacher in her spare time. Well, I was ready for Penny to smack me over the head when she said 'sure, let's do it'… Then…" His grin turned into a frown.

"While you were doing the Snoopy dance of joy, she pulled the rug out from you. What was the condition?" I asked.

"She said that if we have a threesome with one of her friends, it only fair we also have a threesome with one of my friends. Hence…" I pointed all around.

"I'm flattered," I sat back in the living room, "that Penny picked me."

"No, I picked you… Before she could pick Frank."

"Come again?"

"Before she could say with whom, I went and blurted out your name. Have you seen the size of Frank? The guy makes Dwayne Johnson look like a mouse. I want to pork Amanda, and I'm willing to do the whole threesome full circle bit, after all it's only fair, I just want Penny back in one piece. So, you in?"

"Andy," I swigged my cup around, "go home. Watch a porno with Penny and, I don't know, go to couple's therapy."

"You think Penny is ugly?"

I smacked my face, "Andy are you being serious?"

"Is that it?" He huffed. "You won't fuck her cause you think she's ugly?! You think she's a monster. Is that it?"

"Andy, Penny is one hot piece of tail."

"So you'll do it."

"You can't be serious?" I replied. "I am not going to have sex with your wife and you. It will be weird."

"Have you seen Amanda… Come on Nick, take one for the team. It's just been Penny and Karol's handjob. That's it. My whole sexual repertoire. I don't want to die a quasi-virgin. Plus, you have to do it."

"I HAVE to do it?"

"Yeah…"

"And why is that?"

"Cause I told her I'd ask. If you say no, it'll be simply too disrespectful. You wont be able to see her in the face again."

"Ashton Kutcher, come the fuck out. I give up. You got me."

"Dude," went Andy. He skidded up to the edge of his seat, like he was a doctor about to give life threatening news, "if you don't go and sleep with my wife, well, she'll think you don't like her."

"But I do."

"Physically. I mean like a sexual minx. I mean, really, how will you be able to see her in the eyes unless you fuck her? Your friendship will forever be marred by the fact you weren't willing to dick her… and eat her out; not giving her cunnilingus might be the cataclysm that ended your relationship… Nick, give my wife oral sex, otherwise I might not get to see you again."

I tossed Andy out the door and went back to sleep. I was certain that I had woken up in an alternate dimension. My Saturday was turning out to be a very poorly scripted Twilight Zone episode; one written by the crackpot team and edited by Penthouse. I went and got the remaining Wild Turkey and decided to spend the day binge watching Netflix, downing what was left of the bottle. As it turned out, I ended up choking the turkey and spanking the monkey about 3 times thinking about Penny's ass; I had a picture of her in a red two piece bikini that really cracked up the engines.

Ring. Although in hindsight it wasn't really a ring but a weird metallic bing. My cellphones starts doing the Macarena, flashing lights, vibrating all over my night stand. I pray open one of my eye, the other partly shut closed and wired tight by the bottle of Wild Turkey. 1.A.M in the morning. I lunge for the phone, fall off the bed and scramble for the thing. The sound jackhammering me awake. I look at the display. It's either Penny or Jenna Jameson.

"Hello?"

"Why won't you fuck me?"

"Jesus on a tricycle... Really? This again?"

"I though we were friends."

"Penny, It's 1 in the morning. Can we talk about this later? Like I don't know, *never*?"

"Really, that bad?"

"I don't know if you guys are either joking, or you're stoned. Really, I'm at a lost. It's too far fetched," I grumble. "Can't we just leave it? Let's just say you had a laugh at my expense."

"Fine, fine... Andy's birthday is this weekend and I am organizing a night out in town to celebrate."

"Who's coming?"

"The usual gang."

"Is Frank coming?"

"Andy asked me the same damn question. He's a friend, right? Sure, he's coming. Why Is Frank such a big deal?"

"Nothing," Andy had done a number on me. "Text me the details, I'll be there."

"Dinner and a bar or two. Just close friends, so don't bring a date."

"Got it…"

"So, will you fuck me?"

"I'm hanging up now."

I clicked off and went back to sleep.

Andy's birthday arrived. Penny called me and asked me to meet up at their place before going out. We were going to ditch the cars and take a car to the pubs. I bought the funny fuck a bottle of expensive hootch; a Johnny Walker Blue Label that had cost me a dime or two.

"Nicky," he said when he opened the door. Andy was 35 but looked like a well built teen. He had been a track star back in his glory day; not an ounce of fat on in. Everything packed and tight. Imagine Tom Hanks in the 80's but with muscles. He worked out 3 times a week, ran for over an hour and then did some weight training for half an hour more.

"You look like a scarecrow," I said. That was Andy's biggest problem, clothes seem to hand off him. No matter the size, he seemed to always be wearing his parents duds. If you hadn't seen him without a his shirts, you would swear he was malnourished; instead, his body was wound up in steel cables of muscles.

"You really are an asshole.. Cool Bourbon," he snatched the bottle from my hands.

"Bourbon has to be made in the US and the cask can only be used once," Penny corrected him from the kitchen. "That's Scotch… I think. Or Whiskey."

"She's right," I went in a gave her a kiss on the cheek.

Penny was wearing a pair of tight black jeans, a white buttoned blouse covered by an elegant jeans jacket and a pair of low heels. Her 32 years, athletic body and long auburn hair, not to mention her stunning brown eyes - like tiny M&Ms - were rocking the hell out off the whole ensemble. She and Andy were a solid match. She was a bit bigger than him, taller and broader, and shapelier. They reminded me of the DC superhero couple, Mister Miracle and Big Barda. Penny was a viking while Andy was a stage magician.

"Probably taste the same as bourbon," Andy grabbed the bottle.

"He really is a Philistine," Penny said. "It's good to see you."

We exchanged some more pleasantries, googled wether Johnny Walker was Whiskey or Scotch, ate a bag of Doritos - aged, at least 18 year, booze with trans fat truly is the appetizer of giants - and waited for everyone to arrive.

When the crew had assembled, we ordered up a couple of town cars and started the pub crawl. Frank, needed his now freaking car.

"I bet he eats small children," went Andy as Frank ducked into the Land-rover. "Probably hides under a bridge or something."

We had a swell time. It was fantastic. The sort of night out that reminds you why you like being a social creatures and not a lone wolf Unabomber type. The dinner was a five star affair, the company was sublime, the drinks were mouthwatering. Eventually, we called it a night and each of us headed back to their place; a couple of pints in and everyone flew off like roaches to their own hole. Frank stumped out while out glasses shook.

"The Jurassic Park affect," went Jeanne, Andy's sister. "Man, I want to climb that dinosaur."

I gabbed, gobsmacked at her as she gave me a peck on the cheek.

"Someday," she said while walking out the door.

Andy, half in the bag, and Penny, on her way to being drunk, suggested that I - who had started early and was now partly in the hangover stage of the night - take over.

"You're already over the bend… you're the designated adult. Nick, call us an Uber and let's go home for a final nightcap," Andy called out.

On the ride back we congratulated Penny on throwing a great birthday. She wasn't even registering us.

"I'll crack open the bourbon…"

"Scotch," Penny and I screamed.

"Yeah, that, I'll crack it open. It's still early."

I gave in to the birthday boy, and the bottle of expensive booze; I'm easy that way. When the Uber stopped at their place all three of us stumbled up and marched in a line to the apartment.

We skated in. I plumbed down on the couch, Penny went to freshen up and Andy started to fight with the bottle's cap. I was about to get up and help, when a couple of high heel pumps flew across the living room and smashed into the wall. Penny waddled in, tossed her jacket on the backrest and slinked in besides me. She was like a drunken serpent; cool, slinky and a tipsy.

"Andy, I want champagne," she told the birthday boy. Then, as if I wasn't there, she unclamped her bra and jiggled it out from underneath her blouse.

"That's fucking better," she told the room. "Catch…"

And, well, I caught. The thing was black, laced, and it smelled like her; the sort of underwear you put on only for certain special occasions. It felt both cool and extremely hot under my fingers. The metal rims frigid, while the cups, where her nipples had been minutes ago, were pulsating with heat. I turned to her just as Andy came and but down two drink glasses and a brimming champagne flute, and yup, you could see Penny's breast poking the fabric; two perfectly shaped nipples cutting like knife tips the dainty textile. I crossed my legs and stuffed the bra under a cushion.

"Here you go," Andy poured the scotch and the three of us clinked glasses.

"Happy Birthday, big boy," Penny said.

Andy answered her with a well placed kiss. A deep sloppy, passionate, I want to eat you whole, smush that made me blush. It wasn't long, but it was furious; primal and coquettish.

"Did she just give out a little moan?" I asked myself.

You could see color running up Penny's body, her alabaster skin flushed with running blood. A rouge glow painted her cheeks and smeared her lips. In my mind, I imagined her nipple getting harder; the point of each turning into cherries.

"I really should go…"

"Stay a bit," Penny told me.

One drink slowly turned into a second, and by the time we were hitting the third, our already lubricated tongues were punching speed of sound; the amount of bull crap, tall tales and shit splattering the walls was positively staggering.

"I once saw a donkey show," three sips into his second Andy blurred out. "Or maybe it was Furry show… I'm not sure. It was in Miami Beach and that place is surreal."

"Last week, I scratched my boss' car… Right down the middle. The motherfucker deserved it," laughing her ass off Penny confided.

Our tongues were loose, our inhibitions on fire and our guts hungry for what the other offered. We were friends being not only friendly but familial. I was on the floor, rolling like a pig in his own filth, cackling like a madman - Andy has just tried to dance the YMCA blindfolded and with his feet tied - when Penny said: "I am getting bored, let's do something fun."

"Like what?" Asked Andy.

"Let me crack open the closet and see what slithers out," Penny wiggled her tush and flung open than treasure trove. "Monopoly? Nah, I got to work next week. Operations?"

"Used the batteries for the T.V. control," went Andy.

"The one with the ladders? Or Hungry Hungry Hippos?"

"Overthink it, Pen. Just grab some poker cards and I'll shuffle," I told her.

"What game then?"

"I was thinking poker," Penny replied.

"Strip Poker," went Andy.

"Son of a bitch," I interjected. "You two are still on it? Aren't you?"

"What?" Went Penny nonchalantly. "What do you mean?"

"Dammit, the whole let's raise up our freak flag and do a threesome? I wasn't born yesterday."

"Can't we have an innocent game of strip poker with it being an agenda? Really, Nick," went Andy, "it's not a conspiracy."

"So, this isn't about me fucking your wife?"

"Whatever gave you that insidious and nefarious idea?"

"Andy, really, strip fucking poker," then a pair of black jeans hit me on the shoulders. I turned right as Penny was getting up from the floor. She was missing the point and objective of strip poker; the fact that you first had to deal the cards, then lose before slinking out of your clothes. Penny, as it turned out was an over achiever who continually jumped the gun.

"Our ploy is up, Andy, we better come clean," a pair of laced panties, the twins of that bra hiding under the sofa, poked a hole in my mind. The frilly cloth tightly wrapped around two perfectly formed peaches. I scanned Penny, from head to toe, and lingered on her long smooth legs.

"Cat got your tongue," went the wild cat undressing in front of me. Her belly was taught and flat, the landscape of it slowly coming into being as she shrugged off her blouse. Right before her breast made their triumphant entrance, Penny turned and gave us a perfect view of her back. Muscles catching the lamp light, shadows cast on her dimples, each imperfection and natural sway not subtracting from her beauty but adding layers of erotism.

"You like her new tattoo," Andy pointed to a spot right above her right shoulder. "It's a little butterfly."

"Lady bug," went Penny. Then she turned, arms in a cross around her chest, bare breast clutched tight under their embrace. "I also got a belly button ring."

I was swimming, no drowning in my own thoughts, hardly registering the red ruby on her stomach… a tear drop emerald hanging from a chain pointing downward in a lurid yet highly suggestive manner.

"What the fuck?" I mumbled, only to be meet by more flying draperies. I turned, and sure enough, there was Andy, skipping like a toddler and fighting his way out off a pair of boxers. My friend higher than a kite and sporting a bulging erection that could give Frank a run for his money. "Geez," head swindling back to Penny. Her arms were down and a pair of perky gravity defying breast stood like two saluting foot soldiers; they could cut a diamond. I was wrong, the nipple weren't cherry red but light pink. Perfect cups that I knew, from passed experience with other girls, would fit like plumb and ripe apples in my hands.

"Nick," went Andy, "Join the party…"

Andy flew right pass me and practically tackled Penny against the couch. He didn't just hug her, he wrapped himself around her and engulfed every part of his wife. The man was a blur of motions, like one of those flash after effects that produces blurry photos mid action; more than two hands, more than two legs. Penny started moaning as Andy nuzzled her neck and started pinching her breast. She started to stroke him with one hand, the other sliding under her panties and playing with herself.

"Nick," she groaned, "come on… Don't spoil the fun… I'm shaved."

Maybe, it was the alcohol, the drinks running like wildfire through my veins and creating small short-circuits in my brain. Maybe, it was the fact that it had been almost 8 months to the day since I was last with another woman. Maybe, it was the nights intoxicating sway and flow. Or, maybe, and just maybe, I'm really not discounting this fact, it was Penny's magnificent body; small beats of sweat already creating an oily shine over her muscles. It's the sort of question philosopher's could argue about ad infinitum… What was clear, nonetheless, was the irrefutable knowledge that my pants were now two sizes too small and my hands were going apeshit of their own accord.

"That's its buddy," Andy said just before his mouth clamped around Penny's breast. I looked down and, sure enough, my traitorous digits, the two-bit bastards, were unbuckling my belt and getting frisky with with my jeans. I slipped out off my pants and started almost ripping off my shirt.

"That's the body I've been dreaming about," Penny said. Her hand pressing against the back of Andy's head, smothering him against her nipples; moving and commanding her husband's motions. She stared at me, her eyes engulfing every inch of my chest, there was a look of hunger in her eyes. A look that redefined the concept of lust. A started to walk towards that magnet; a moth to flame.

"Nick," she bit her lips, Andy, no doubt had just taken a love bite at her nipples, "Nick," once more she started, as a neared her, boxers still on, "Nick, you've been keeping up… Still the same jock body."

I knew she was lying, I'd gained, since those glory days, a couple of pounds. My gut wasn't as flat and tight. Monday night football practice taking a backseat to Friday night happy hours. Still, I managed to have a nice, overall, decent body. Everything was were it had to be, nothing was out of place. Back when I was scoring touchdowns I looked like Chris Evans about to do an action film. Blond hair slicked back. Blue eyes sparkling with innocence. A gun-ho attitude and the muscles to back up that claim. Now, almost 15 years afterwards, that blond mane is starting to get gray streaks on the side. Those blue eyes aren't as deep and innocent, as radiant as before. In the mirror, each morning, I see that life has taken some of their luster away. That moxie has been replaced, not by pessimism but by a calm that evaluates each battle. Before I would have gone to war with a passion and a zeal for just about any cause, trivial or not, now I chose my skirmishes. Those muscles, they're still their, clinging to a frame that gets increasing amounts of aches each time it hits the gym. That six pack, those cannon size forearms are still there, maybe not as big as before, but they're there.

I got next Penny, inches from her mouth, unaware mental what I wanted to do, what I wanted her to, in full knowledge instinctual what my body desired. My hands reached down and started to peel off my boxers.

"Stop," Penny said. She reached over but her palm against my groin and through the flimsy fabric she began to fell my rigid shaft. Now it was my turn to moan. I closed my eyes in ecstasy and rapidly flick them on again. Her black finger nails, her pale beautiful skin, her delicate fingers curled around the contours of my cock was an image I wanted to tattoo in my mind.

"Not yet, just let me imagine it for a few more seconds," Penny told me.

Andy, meanwhile, had started to glide away from his wife's ravaged breast. He was slowly sliding down her body. Kissing, nippling, pressing his fingers against her. Jolts, you could practically see them, were washing over Penny, making her arch her back, making her moan in delight, making her flesh turn to goosebumps and her hair respond.

Penny reached below my boxers, never taking them off, slipping her hand over the rim the very second Andy's mouth zeroed in on her panties. I could hear Andy, his hot breath glancing over Penny's pubis. He started to pull her last piece of clothing off her wanton and gleaning body. He pulled from the back, his fingernails leaving small scratch marks over her ass. Almost as if they were reading each other's mind, years of marriage will do that to a person, Penny started to draw down my boxers. She smiled and grinned, like a malnourished wolf who had just spotted easy prey, the very second my cock finally made it's entrance onto the stage.

"It's a bit thicker than Andy's," she said.

"Yeah," down below a voice added, "but mine's longer."

"Best of two worlds," Penny flung off my boxers and wrapped her fingers around my shaft. I could see she was testing the width. "You know," my erect dick in my best friend's wife's sexy hand, "you could, I don't know every-so-often say something."

And, after being the mute in that bizarre porn film, I finally did, "Penny, suck my cock."

And just like that, without any need of further encouragement, Penny, sweat innocent, Penny. Penny, my friend - perhaps my only real opposite sex friend. Penny who I had known for so many years. Penny, the love of Andy's life. Penny who I had seen cry and curse. Penny who I once had to take home because she was so drunk. Penny who I copied off in high-school. That very same, almost saintly Penny, opened her mouth and swallowed me whole. She deep-throated until she almost choked on my shaft.

"That's my cue," Andy said. I looked and down he went, his tongue flicking over Penny's clit, his finger going in and out of hers, yup it was shaved, pussy.

Penny picked up her pace, engulfing me, giving me the best blowjob in my life right as Andy went and cemented his lips over her cunt. She moaned, and I could feel her vocal chords vibrating down my shaft. It was slippery, wet, with the right amount of spit and nasty. She but her hands around my balls and started playing with them. Andy, was making her tremble. She pulled away from it, a line of spit and pre-cum running from my cocks tip to her lips and looked straight up at me. We locked eyes.

"God," she said, "do you have any idea I many times I've masturbated thinking about this?" Then, she went back to work.

Each time I was about to climax, Penny would pull out, and let me calm down. Meanwhile, Andy did the same thing. Each time Penny was about to explode, he'd stop pleasuring her and start rubbing her belly. Penny began sucking my testicles. Putting them in her mouth, I reached down and started, I had seen it in porn movie, I really had no script, slapping her cheek with my erect dick. Then, she, screamed. I could feel she was moments away from having her first orgasm. Andy was below not only sucking her like a pro' but also finger fucking; giving her a combo that I knew drove women wild.

"I want to cum. I want you to cum. Where do you want to finish?"

Without hesitation, I said, "on your tits."

She took me in one last time. With a blinding ferocity her lips started to go up and down my shaft. Ot was sloppy. It was wet. It was amazing. Penny grabbed my ass and used my whole body as leverage, she pushed me towards her throat and basically stabbed herself with my cock. In, out, in, out. Gagging on it. One second she was kissing and giving my tip a nip, the next she had her whole mouth firmly placed like a suction cup around the base of my shaft.

"I'm going to cum," I whispered in one of her thrusts. The sensations were too much, the sights too mind-blowing, everything was making my body overload. Andy started to lap his wife's pussy faster and faster. He was focused all his attention on her clit. Penny grabbed my balls, pressed harder and right at the very second I saw her shuttering, right at the very second I felt her climax, the ripple of her mute moan of delight traveling like shockwaves over my cock, I let go… I exploded into her throat. Penny pulled out immediately, semen hanging like confetti from her lips, she arched her back and pointed my throbbing penis at her chest. I was discharging all over the place, my knees weak, my eyes foggy. She guided me and painted her upper body. Splashed on her belly. Splashes on her perky tits. Splashes on her neck. My body jerking with the spasms of my incredible climax; Penny keeping up with the beat, her own rhythm in synch with mine.

"Whoa," Penny went, "you were really packing. Now that's a load."

I looked at her naked, incredible, body and realized that I had painted a rather naughty Jackson Pollock all over her fleshy canvas. I stood back, right as Andy came up and started to kiss Penny passionately. His tongue darting in and out of Penny's lips. His teeth taking little love bites and pulling. Only now, three things popped into my mind. One, I hadn't even kissed Penny yet. Two, Andy, as bizarre as it seemed ,didn't even care that he was kissing his wife, rolling around in her mouth, fondling her body, tracing his wanton hands over her flesh, while also tasting and feeling up my cum. And, finally, more importantly, I was superfluous to the whole scenario. Yes, Penny was positively turned on by me, or at least I thought so, but Andy and her were so in line, so connected that I really wasn't that critical, just a prop for their love making, a toy, a dildo with a heartbeat. Under other circumstance it might have felt cheap, but here, Andy cradling his wife's ass with one hand, his fingers once more massaging her clit, while he licked her cheeks and stroked his cock against her left thigh, I understood that I was helping them scratch an item off their bucket list… and getting some free booty in return; it really was a win win situation.

"I'm going to get a drink," I said and, noticing that they didn't even register me, headed towards the kitchen. "We're out of, well, everything."

I stood in front of the fridge, frozen by the sight of my cock, already getting hard once more. Was that lipstick on it? I grabbed it, inspected my tool and, yes, it was ruby red lipgloss; Penny's shade. Streaks of it smeared up and down my shaft. What a night. I started to get re-hydrated when the pounding started. Instantly, I knew what was going on, and, instantly, I flew into the living room not wanting to miss a thing.

Andy was riding Penny. Half his wife's body hanging from the sofa's armrest, her fingers digging into the cushions for dear life. Her frame rigid and plastered, breasts squeezed under her weight against the furniture. Andy, naked behind her, pulling at her hair, while simultaneously pushing her shoulders down.; pinning her in a wrestling move. Penny's ass grinding against groin. Andy's cock going in and out with jackhammer fluidity. He wasn't just taking her from behind, he was braking her in two. I got closer, my dick once more getting hard and, to my astonishment, noticed that Andy was fucking his wife anally. Penny really wasn't the sort of girl you're imagine was into that… Then, penny wasn't the sort of girl you'd imagine in this scenario. Not the sort of girl how knew what a cockhold was let alone the sort of girl who be the protagonist of a threesome.

"Holy shit," I said memorized by Penny's face, a mix of pain and pleasure as Andy sodomized her with predatory glee. Tears streaming down her cheeks. Eyes clamped shut. Was he hurting her? Was Andy assaulting his wife?

"Harder," Penny shrieked, "harder…" I guessed that answered that. Her fingernails almost ripping open the velvet cushions. "Don't you dare fucking stop…" She smashed her face down on the sofa, Andy having taken her word as gospel. Then, she began to drown out her screams as Andy pulled his cock out of her ass and started impaling her in rapid motions; the man coming in from behind with force and deliberation. Andy pushed her whole body against the sofa, got up on one leg and went to town. It was violent, brutal, almost a rape, but his wife was having a grand time.

I started, unconsciously, to masturbate in front of them. Tracing my hand over my shaft, my cock still wet and warm from the violent deep throat fuck it had just gotten. Andy was panting like a dog, rivulets of sweat cascading from his brow onto Penny's naked back. He grabbed her hips and, I still don't know how, mid thrust he went and flipped her.

Now, penny was sitting on top of her husband; Using Andy as a chair. Both her knees buckled tight, her chest bowed and tilted, her arms wrapped against Andy's neck and nape. Her breast were bobbing up and down. I let go of my dick and went in. I began sucking her ripe nipples, bitting them, licking them. I felt her fingers scratch my back. None of us were even saying a word. The time for dirty talk had expired, we were in the moment being swept up by the sheer animal fervor that clung like a miasma to the room. I tasted the salty tang of my cum and her sweat.

"Oh, God," Penny moaned. Her heartbeat exploding. Andy panted, his muscles glinting as sweat oiled them up. He started to bite down on her neck.

"Don't you dare cum yet," Penny told him. "Not yet." Then she slowed her rhythm. Andy calmed down. He no longer thrusted and poked his wife's ass but let her rest. "You're so fucking hard."

Then, as if the whole thing had been choreographed, and after so many nights of them fantasying about it it probably was, Andy's hands clasped Penny's knees. He started to part them apart, his legs cracking open his wife, exposing her… a written invitation. I knew what I was being offered, and seeing that pink shaved cavern I didn't have to be told twice.

"My turn," I said gliding down and putting my lips on her labia. I felt my best friend's balls against my chin. We were so close, when I pulled and looked at Penny's clit I could see part of Andy's penis, the other half enveloped by his wife's cunt. I started to eat her out. For the next 15 minutes I licked my best friend's wife's vagina like I had done to no other woman on Earth. My school buddy was meanwhile anally pleasuring that same grant lady. Penny pushed my head against her clit. She would clamp her knees, mid spasm, against my ears only for Andy to come and once more pull them apart. The son of bitch wanted her at his mercy. He was offering his wife to me like a trinket… like a lollypop. Penny came about 3 times. Each time she would shutter and try to get out of the bind Andy had put her in. Each time, no doubt too sensible, she would try to extricate herself. And, each time, Andy would snap down his hands on her shoulder and brace her back into place.

"No more," Penny would scream. Andy would hold her like a vice back against his cock. "Too much," Andy would have none of it. "No more… You're killing me… God, I can't come anymore… God…."

Then, Andy, would disregard her pleas for mercy, and stick his palm against her mouth; silencing her cries. "You wanted this, you fucking whore… Next week, I'm going to do the same to Amanda… Look at Nick and take notes, study his technique, cause you're going to need it come Monday." With those few words, Penny climaxed a fourth time. Her eyes shut, no longer a human but a doll that wanted, needed, to be used and dirtied. She stopped fighting and started riding the wave.

"Nick," she said. I looked up, her face a glossy sheen on perspiration, "Nick, come here." I went and I finally got my first kiss. Our tongues fighting for space in each other's mouth.

"Do you like the way you tastes?" I asked her.

She winked, and responded: "I could ask you the same thing." Then, she grabbed my cock once more and said: "stick it in… Fuck me."

Andy heard her and once more pried her pussy wide open for me. I slapped her tights and her clit, Penny gave off a small moan with each playful hit. I got on my knees, and…

"Jesus," Penny went. Her call for divine intervention the bell that signaled the proverbial cherry on top of this pornscape. I went in softly first, just the tip, then little by little slid all the way in.

"I can feel both of you," Penny said and I realized that I too could feel both of them. Penny's wet, slippery pussy wrapped around my cock and, inside, a small thin wall of flesh separated me from Andy. The palpitations of both their heartbeats reverberating in that small space. Whenever Andy moved, I could sense his presence… every-so-often I could actually feel his penis pushing against that wall; his wife's anal cavity stuffed.

We began to double penetrate Penny. My face pressed agains her breasts, her hands anchored to my back, my dick forcing itself into her. I could feel every time Penny came, her pussy getting for seconds tight against me. Each new climax only shortened the time span for the next one. Andy had been working his wife for more than 45 minutes straight. It really was amazing. He was either high on something or my old friend had a thing or two to teach me.

  Andy pushed us off the couch and we felt on the floor. The cold ceramic clashing with my warm back. Penny rearranged herself on top of me. Her breast almost ripped out from my hungry mouth and now dangling against my sensitive chest. Her nipples pinging off mine. She dug her finger nails into my hair and pulled me towards her, "I've wanted you for so long." Then she started to devour my tongue.

  Andy, meanwhile, got on top of his wife. I could feel part of his weight on fall on me. I could smell him just inches away. I could feel his testicles hitting mine, his hands glancing off my body. I wasn't gay, I wasn't bi, but the pleasure and jolt of electricity I felt whenever my best friend's fingers trailed up and down my belly was sublime. His nails digging into the sides of my rib cage got me harder. Penny, instinctually, got wind of it.

  "You know," she whispered into my ear, "he really wants to suck you off." I was speechless. "Maybe some other day, or some other time. That would really turn me on." The though of Andy, his lips around my cock, while Penny played with herself, made me almost cum. "Damn, that got you really stiff," Penny said.

  "I'm almost there," Andy told us. Had he heard his wife?

"Me too," I went locking eyes with Andy. In for a penny, no pun intended, in for a pound.

Penny braced herself, clawed at my shoulders, got up and screamed, enough for the neighbors to hear, "I'm a fucking cumdump!"

Andy and I let go simultaneously. Penny made small animal noises as we filled her up. I could feel cum dripping out of her pussy back onto my cock. I could feel Andy's penis giving off small spasms as dribbles of his semen flowed down his wife's crack and mingled with mine. I wanted to pull out, but Penny, mid orgasm, held me in place and rode me a bit more. My toes curdling up. My groin a mix of liquids. My mind racing.

We finally plopped onto the sides, Penny in the middle of us. Each beaten and raw. I stared at her heaving body, her breath coming in punches. I stared at Andy's wet soaked frame, his cock humid and still partly erect. I stared at my own body, I looked like a rain soaked puppy. I closed my eyes.

"Well, that was interesting," Penny said. "Really something to remember."

"Damn straight," Andy went.

"Holy shit," I countered. "I'd be willing to do it again."

"Who the fuck said we were done," Andy told me.

I felt a hand grabbing my cock. Penny already getting frisky. I felt my dick take notice. I wanted to say that was all for the night, but my anatomy was doing something all together different.

Penny started stroking my hair. She pushed against my tight, her wet labia rubbing up and down my leg muscles. Se started to moan once more. Really, Penny could go on for hours. She started to lick my checks, my chest, my arms. My penis getting aroused; the stroking motions getting that friend back into the field. Penny bit down on my chest, and played with my nipples. She clawed both sides of my body with her nails. The left and right at the same time. I moaned and grabbed her arms, her oily shoulders, and ran my fingers along them. I was hard again. I couldn't believe it. I was once more ready for action. The stroking had… The stroking? What the fuck. I popped open my eyes.

There was something off. Penny was scratching my rib cage… both sides. I wasn't imagining it. She was also, somehow, giving me a hand job? No, impossible. I swerved up and, yes, there was Penny, her lips clapped around my nipples, her limps wrapped around me. I gabbed further down, past her dropping hair, past her new tattoo, past her spine, past her incredible butt checks, and gasped.

Andy was the one giving me a hand job. He got up, moved towards my cock. Penny saw my bewildered and partly aroused expression, put her hand against my chest and pushed me back down on the floor. "I told you what he wanted…"

Then I just laid back and, well, in for penny in for a pound…

CARIBBEAN GET AWAY

"The first time I had a threesome was in high school. It really wasn't so much a threesome, it was more or less a clusterfuck. It was with my best friend and my step brother. My parents had been divorced for about 5 years, and mom finally decided to get re-married. She got hitched to a Costa Rican man-child. The guy that was the iconic of latin heartthrob. All fun. All lusty body. All great attitude. All smoke and mirrors. Good for a good time but not for the long haul. My mom was 56, this guy was 35. Right out off the gate you just knew what she wanted. Sex. She basically formalized a giggalo relationship. I really didn't care. The guy was cheating on her the very second the ink was dry on the marriage certificates. She knew what she was getting into. My dad had left her a huge sum of money from the settlement and, well, in hindsight I could defiantly see the advantages of having a private booty call on speed dial. After all, my dad was a stereotypical household who had dumped my mom for, and I kid you not, a receptionist named Jennifer, 25 year younger than him, who had once been a 'dancer' by the name of Bambi; it was such a cliche that I was embarrassed to even talk about it. So, when my mom started hooking up with her version of

Bambi, and by the sounds she made at midnight, proving that menopause did wonders for your sex life I really couldn't blame her.

Anyway, it turned out the man child had a child… And it turned out that the kid was a spitting image of his father only with youth and better genetics thrown in the mix. Juan, that was his name, was the whole package. His mother had been a Colombian beauty pageant queen. She looked like a better version of that actress from Modern Family… and the man-child was basically Ricky Martin mixed with Enrique Iglesias. The kid had everything a young adolescent girl could want. He had the smoking good looks; the sort you only see in album covers. Penetrating chocolate eyes that could cut you to the bone if you let them. A mane of black unruly hair. That latin thing superpower that, no matter the climate, no matter the season, no matter if it was 20 below zero and the sun had last been seen a month ago, allowed them to somehow maintain a perpetual cooper tan. You added those quirks to the fact that he had a swimmer's body and a foreign accent plucked straight out of an erotic novel and the guy was basically a wrong decision waiting to crystallize. I was 17 at the time and he was 16. I knew he was trouble, the good kind, right from the day we meet. Juan looked me up and down, peeked my on the cheek - cause that's how they say hello in Latin America - and whispered in my ear 'that tattoo is really hot.' He was referring to a Cheshire Cat - from Alice in Wonderland - that I had on my thigh; the same thigh that was partly covered by Daisy Duke cut offs… the kid had really inspected me. I blushed.

The first few months were casual pass by. He would jump in the pool whenever I was sunbathing. His tight little swimwear perfectly framing his, as it turned out, rather impressive tool. He would come into my room, not really knocking and ask for something. Getting looks at my pajamas, my bras hanging on the chair and once a mental snapshot of me partly dressed. I'd scream my head off and slam the door shut in his face, and then I'd masturbate thinking of where it could have lead. My friends just wanted to eat him up. They'd stop by the house for no reason and casually ask: 'is your step-brother home?'

Then, one day things took a turn. I was at school, and Moira comes up to me and starts gossiping at blinding speed. It turns out Juan went out on a date with this other girl, Karen. Karen, apparently wasn't a shy girl. They ended up fucking… and worst, the son of bitch, as it turned out was an excellent lay. All the girls were talking about it. The rumor mill was in full swing and suddenly Juan had a bit more cache than just a stunning body; it seemed the little devil knew his way around in the sack. My step brother was fast becoming my go-to fixture whenever I need to find some relief or simply couldn't go to sleep. By the way things were sharping up, It seemed he was fast becoming the poster child for erotic fantasies for every girl in the school.

And there he was, all day and every night, going around the house like he owned the place. Sometimes with his shirt off. Other times just his swimming trunks and that shape I already talked about. I was starting to get cramps in my wrist from playing around with myself so much. One time, I actually caught him skipping out of shower, wet and steaming, nothing but a towel wrapped around his waist. I turned, 'sorry, though I was alone,' and put my hand over my eyes. He strolled straight into his room, but not before I managed to peek between my fingers and get a quick glance at his ass. The bastard, I swear he did it on purpose, had allowed a slip of cloth to skate open. His buns, one of the two, was touching the night air… he was flashing me. My nipples went erect in a second flat. The sight plus the air condition cranking my hormones to overdrive. I went straight into the bathroom and took a long shower. We had a jacuzzi, one of the perks of my mom's settlement, and that day the electric bill broke the roof; I gave the jets one hell of a workout.

'You know,' went Moira one day, 'he totally wants you.'

'Who?'

'Your step brother…'

'He's a guy, he'd probably fuck the lunch lady.'

'Probably, but I see the way he sometimes gets caught looking at your cleavage. I swear it's like he's mesmerized.'

I blushed, brushed Moira off and started wearing low cut blouses around the house. Most of the time without a bra. And, also, I suddenly became incredibly clumsy around him. 'Oops, I swear I don't know what is up with me. It must be the new cream I'm wearing. Keep dropping everything.' I'd bend and then I'd get a nice frisson of sexual energy when I saw Juan's pants getting tighter.

The tension around the house was palpable. I was masturbating constantly thinking of him and, as I later discovered, he in turn was making it an organized sport jerking off to a picture he had taken off my Facebook feed. I pic' of me and Moira at the beach, both wearing matching bikinis and goofing around with ice cream cones.

Things started to go sour in my mom's relationship. You could practically read the writing on the wall. Man-child was fucking it up big time. The child part was beating, senselessly, the man part. If you added that, with any luck, my mom's fuck fest was about to expire with the circumstances that I was month's away from skipping town and going of to UCLA, you suddenly had an result that made my wet dream turn to dust. Juan and I were about to go our separate ways, and frankly I was too damn horny to leave it like that. I wanted to fuck him silly, period.

Moira and I started building up our won conspiracy. She would have sold her soul for a pass at Juan. Her friendship and mine was a bit complicated. She had been my first real kiss. She had been my confident. And, more importantly, she had been my first real lover. I had lost my virginity a year ago to some random guy I meet at a school rally, but to years prior Moira and I had our own school-girl fling. We were at least kissing buddies, at most friends with benefits; we rarely cashed in on those benefits, but once a month - maybe even twice - we'd have a sleep-over and rarely did we sleep.

We needed to bait the hook; to chum up the surf with something irresistible that Juan simply couldn't ignore. And, frankly, Moira and me were more than yummy… we had fins to the left and fins to the right on a daily basis.

My mom was out of town for the first summer weekend. Her and the man-child, or the boy-toy, had gone to Cancun. Either a desperate gambit to safe the relationship or one last sexual free-for-all. They were in an all-inclusive, drinking margaritas and fucking their brains out. Meanwhile, Moira, Juan and myself were back home… sipping Buds' and also about to fuck our brains out; the apple really doesn't fall far from the tree.

Moira had come to 'study' while Juan was doing some exercises in the pool. It was past 9, and already we were acting like total brats. We'd skip out onto the yard, screeching like teens and piss him off. Moira, wearing her skimpiest black bikini with red lace, a little two piece suit that barely covered her ass and tucked her tiny yet perky breast, flaunted her tail up and down the pool area. Moira was a thing to behold. She was the poster child for the Suicide Girl brand; raven hair with scarlet colored tip, pale skin, a thin long vampire like body, blue eyes with flecks of emerald, and about a dozen tattoos. I could have stared at her for hours, and I sometimes did. Her art work; her whole flesh a graffiti canvas. She was what I liked to call goth chick, painted black nails, nose ring and a fashion sense bought off the rack at Hot Topic. What really drove guys wild, and me on more than one occasions while she was going down on my pussy, was the tongue stud. She started to flick her tongue in and out at Juan, making sure the piercing was visible. Juan couldn't take her eyes off her. Meanwhile, I was dancing, my blond hair going up and down, the beat of techno funk coursing through my body. I grabbed Moira by her hips and invited her to party. I was making sure Juan could see that I was tracing her body with my finger nails. We were giving him a show. He stopped doing his routine and just stood there at the rim of the pool memorized by the act. We kept it for awhile; typical stuff guy's dream about and jerk off to in their room… we might as well had have been on a mattress about to start a pillow fight in our Victoria Secret's underwear.

    One thing lead to another and soon Moira and I were both inside the pool. It was getting late, the six packs were all but gone and you could see, with the pool's underwater lights, that Juan had a huge hard on. I decided to crank it up and right in front of Juan I casually ripped the upper part of Moira's bikini. Then, maybe it was the booze, maybe it was the situation, or maybe it was just the fact that as much as I wanted to fuck Juan, the bastard couldn't hold a candle to Moira. I swung Moira around and started to kiss her. She in turn pressed against me, her head just above the water, her breast brushing against mine and opened up her mouth; I started to probe her with my tongue… our hands picking up the pace and followed suit. My top half was clasped off and discarded. Moira pushed me into the shallow end of the pool, waist deep, and started sucking my breast. I held onto the rim of the pool, in full blown ecstasy… Where was Juan? I thought. Then, as if my question had rung a dinner bell, I knew exactly where Juan was. I felt something enter me from behind, the fabric from my bottom half slipped to one side. I gasped, Moira dug in her teeth and gave me a long love bite, pulling at my nipple. I felt the thrust a second time. This time deeper and with more force. I turned and realized that my step-brother was finger fucking me. First with one long finger, slippery and lubricated by the pool's water, then with two. Moira, meanwhile had taken my hand and guided it towards her pussy. She went, turned around, and pressed her back against my chest. She somehow wiggled out of what was left of her bikini, pushed her ass against me and I knew exactly what she wanted. While Juan was pounding my vagina with his fingers, I went and finger fucked my best friend. I tried to mimic Juan's movements. When he pulled out, I pulled out of Moira. When he plunged his digits in, I did the same. When it was hard, I made Moira cry in pain. When it was soft, I caressed Moira's clit and made her purr like a cat.

    I had already climaxed when I felt something strong and meaty brush against my thigh. A swim trunk was tossed like a wet bomb outside the pool. I went, let go of Moira's snatch and turned. My hands disappeared under the water and found Juan's erect cock. I started to stroke it. Then Moira game into the game, clamping against me. She too started to stroke it. We were giving Juan the mother of all hand job. Even with our four hands running up and down his shaft we still had plenty of room; the kid had been blessed.

Moira, I still remember it to this day, whispered in my ear, 'I want you to watch.' Then, she pushed me aside and patted the outside of the pool. Juan pulled himself up in one fluid motion, his muscles tightening to steel in that second. He sat on the lip of the pool, legs dangling, cock erect and a goofy mischievous smile. Moira spread his legs and gave me the most erotic show I had seen in my life. She started to go down on him. It started out as a blowjob and quickly turned into something else. Juan moaned, his eyes going white and said, 'sis you want to give it a turn?' I was going towards her, when Moira stopped me. She turned, 'she can't, she's mine… Go and wait for me by the stairs.'

I went by the stairs, took off my last shred of clothing off and sat on down. I spread my legs, and began to play with myself. Moira saw me, grabbed Juan's hand and put it on the back of her head, then she made him push her against his cock. She wanted to be face-fucked, and more importantly, she wanted me to see her getting face-fucked; I came a second time. Moira went down on Juan's massive tool, gagging at it as Juan took the hint, and in less than 7 minutes, Juan was coming her mouth. She turned, left him there liked trash, spasming from the release and came to be. She kissed me passionately, Juan's juices still cupped inside her, and we traded spit, tongues and my step-brother's cum. Then she swallowed what was left, climbed out of the pool, and grabbed my hand. She escorted me to a lawn chair, I saw Juan getting up and following. She lay face up on the chair, lounged on it and drew her knees up and opened for me. I went and started kissing her legs, her feet, her inner thighs and finally her pussy. I stayed there, and once more practiced what we had perfected all those long nights while our parent's were asleep and we were suppose to be doing our homework. I started to eat her out as Juan came from behind and without any preamble stuck his once more erect cock into me. I had never had someone as big. Aside from Moira, I had only been with two more sexual partners. Unlike Moira, both were male. They were clumsy and their dicks not something you'd write home about. Juan on the other hand was thick, he was long, but it was the girth that was really giving me new sensations. I felt it press against part of my labia that no other lover had explored. I was being stuffed, about to explode, by something awe- inspiring.

 Moira was looking over my shoulder, her knees pressed against my ears as Juan was fucking me like the little slut I was. She said, 'you know, she masturbates thinking about you almost every night. Has a stuff teddy bear she rubs against her clit.' She said, 'I once fucked her with a vibrator I bought, right up there in her room, and all she could say while cumming was your name.' She said, 'she probably wants to fuck you and your dad at the same time.' I didn't know it, but as I nodded, I realized that yes, I wanted the man-child to pound my pussy while I sucked his kid's cock. She said, 'she really is a filthy little whore.' Statements turned to questions, and Moira asked, 'have you jerked off thinking of your step-sister's cunt?' 'Yes…' Juan answered. She asked, 'have you jerked off often thinking of her tits… maybe cumming on them?' 'Yes…' Juan answered. She asked, 'what's one of the worst things you've done while imagining your step-sister giving you a blowjob?' Juan answered, 'stole one of dirty her panties and jerked off in her bedroom into it. I smelled of her cunt and ass.' Juan answered. That made push back and demand he fuck me deeper. Moira grabbed my hair and pushed me with the same ferocity I had demanded of Juan against her clit. She moaned and she asked, 'would you fuck her with your dad?' Half a second of hesitation, and then Juan answered, 'only if were in on it.' I came right there. Juan exploded inside my pussy, pulled out - luckily I was on the pill - and drenched my back. Moira screamed and came in my mouth.

      The night bore on. We must have fucked until the roasters came home. I need electrolytes from cumin so much. We did it everywhere around the house. I held Moira against the kitchen counter and guided Juan's cock into her. In my bedroom, I sat on Moira's face while I gave Juan a blowjob. In the living room we took turns kissing as Juan fucked one of us, took his cock out and went to town on the other. In the shower, while I was sleeping on the bed, I managed to get a glimpse of Moira riding Juan's cock. In the study, Moira pulled out a strap-on she had bought and Juan jerked off on my dad's old corporate chair while Moira tried it out for the first time on me. And finally, in the morning, an hour before our parents came back home, Moira took me to their bedroom and tied my hands and put a rag in my mouth. 10 minutes later I was desecrating that space. I was being anally manhandled by Juan… The kid popping my ass' cherry, while Moira fucked me with her back strap on. I was being double penetrated… Moira, all the while laughing like a loon at my tears of pain and delight, while she narrated the plan she was cooking up for a full blown orgy with Juan's dad."

Amanda

FRANK'S WILD YEARS

Frank in 4 words: HE'S. A. SCARY. MOTHERFUCKER.

Frank's hold on ambient energy, his grasp on the day to day mechanics of physics and human perception were at best described by the movie *"Desperado."* Right at the beginning, of that film, Steve Buscemi drones into Steve Buscemi mode. He starts giving this whole long drawn out monologue, frightening the living daylights from both the audience and the players in the scene.

"I'm just glad to be alive right now. I was up a few towns away- you know Saragosa? I was visiting a bar there, not unlike this one. They serve beer, not quite as good as this, but close. And I saw something you wouldn't believe. I'm sitting there, see, small table all by myself. Now this bar, it's full of real low-lives. I mean, not like this place here. No, I mean bad. Like they were up to no good, know what I'm sayin'? Anyway, I'm all by myself, I like it that way. Meanwhile, things are going on... under the table kinds of things. Not too obvious, but, not too secret, either. So, I'm sitting there, and in walks the biggest Mexican I have ever seen. Big as shit. Just walks right in like he owns the place. Now, nobody knew quite what to make of

him, or quite what to think. There he was and in he walked. He was dark, too. I don't mean dark-skinned. No, this was different. It was as if he was always walking in a shadow. I mean every step he took towards the light, just when you thought his face was about to be revealed, it wasn't. It was as if the lights dimmed, just for him."

Frank had the same effect, only in broad daylight. It didn't matter the time, it didn't matter wether of not the sun was out, it really didn't matter the season. Whenever you recalled your meeting with Franks, you're brain would somehow add a layer of myst or shadows to the whole affair. You could have been at a children's party, mid-noon, eating birthday cake while a clown made ballon animals in the background, but that night when you're reliving it, your basic instinct for survival would add a haze, like black cloud to the whole affair the second you strolled up to Frank's and said: "hey, buddy, how you doin'?"

He was a man of few words. Huge and bulky, the sort of frame that had to duck and tilt sideway in order to enter a room. He made mountains look like hills. His skin had a perpetual tan or reddish copper sheen. You couldn't really tell where his ancestors had come from. He had that exotic mix of races that would always stump a person. Was he Spanish? Was he Samoan? Was he Native American? Was he from Africa? Was he from the Caribbean?

"I heard he's a descended from the Patagones. From Argentina. The Patagones? Huge native people of the region, practically giants that roamed was is now called Patagonia."

"Naw, he's from Hawaii or the Polynesia. Can't you see the Dwayne in his blood?"

"The Rock looks like a pebble compared to Franks."

"Heard that's not even his real name…"

And that was the thing about Franks, no one was willing to swear on the bible and claim anything as a verifiable truth. The man was a mystery, wrapped up in an enigma, stuffed into a pandora's box and, then, pinched up with razor wire… electrified at that. The guy was bad news on an epic scale. His best friends Nick and Andy were as oblivious as to the nature of Franks as anybody else. If they were asked how the met the big guy, both would have given completely different stories. Penny, meanwhile, simply said when poked and prodded: "He just showed up one day…"

And here's the thing, Penny was constantly being asked about Franks. The second he'd walk in a room, all the girls would turn and you could practically hear panties dropping like lead lined parachutes on the floor. Franks was a sight to behold. All muscles. No, more like muscles stacked on top of muscles. Shoulders tied to back that could lift a Land-rover. A bald shinny head and neat cropped bear that covered his face; his chin chilled from marvel. Tattoos that ran up his arms and dashed out his neck collar. Legs and thighs like oak trees. Dark brown eyes with midnight black pupils. The sort of stare you got from predators. Everything looked like a toy in his hands; tire irons like chop-sticks, liter bottles like airline booze. Anatomically, every girl, and some men, could see, just by what was on display, that he was proportional… which, by the fact that he had to have his shoes costumed made, each feet the size of a VW beetle, spoke volumes about other outré bodily parts. "I wouldn't recommend it," Penny would always tell the newcomers. "It's like playing with fire and sticking your hands in the flame, while brushing your teeth with gasoline."

Her warnings constantly falling on deaf hears. Lambs to the slaughter. Moths to the mosquito light. The gazelles would swarm around Franks, trying to catch his attention; not being the crocodile waiting just below the watering hole's surface. If they were lucky, he'd brush them off… If not, well…

"Franks ruins women."

"That bad?" Asked Jeanne, Andy's sister.

"Depends of your definition of 'bad'. Franks ruins a girl the same way driving a Jaguar ruins you for every other car out there. There's a before and then there's an after. Had an office colleague once, Franks loves redheads, that looked like Scarlett Johansson. Well, dyed up hair… Goth looking. Gives me the willies, her and Amanda had a weird thing together. Well, back to the plot. Franks take her home. Wink, wink. I didn't see her back at work for about a week… and she was walking funny."

"God…"

"Anyway, Franks is a one night kind of guy. At least that's what Andy tells me. He's good for a fling but hates relationship. Always clear about it from the get-go. A gentleman that way. It's your fault if you think you can domesticate him. They part their separate ways. Scarlett starts dating this other guy, amazing guy, a real looker. She gets hitched. On her bachelor party she's drunk off her ass. She starts telling everybody how her soon to be husband is basically a magician in the sack. The guy makes her cum every time they're together. She actually pick ups a Pint class, and stuffs it on top of another… 'that big' she goes. We're all jealous. Someone asks. 'best lay ever?' And you want to know what she said?"

"Let me guess, Franks?"

"Bingo! Scarlett went and got hitched to a Jaguar or a Porsche, only to realize that Franks was like one of those flying cars from The Jetsons. The guy is a fucking Unicorn."

"Where does he life?" A new goal in life popping inside Jeanne's head.

"You know… I'm really not sure…"

The night of Andy's birthday, Franks went and got plowed in each one every bar Penny brought him into. The guy was a guy's guy. He could hold his liquor like the best of sailors. 4 pitchers of IPA in and Franks barely had a buzz. He looked at the birthday boy and smiled, a crack that was barely registering on his lips.

"Glad you're having fun, big man," Penny patted him on the back and handed him a fifth pitcher; a creamy stout this time. "Karaoke's next."

He liked Penny. She was one of the few dames out there that actually understood him. She didn't bother him and was a friend while doing it. Andy and Nick, meanwhile, were the perpetual adults somehow always trying to slip back into their childhood. Grown man who did their level best to try and catch a fatal doze of Peter Pan Syndrome. That was the way the modern world worked. 45-year-olds with iPods, going around town on motorized skateboards; going to work with a Captain America t-shirt and a copy of Harry Potter under their arms.

"Dude," went Nick, "It's Bohemian Rhapsody… Come on Franks, we need a 'Galileo'."

Franks grunted and got up. Nick and Andy were muttonheads, but they were his muttonheads. That and it was Queen, you simply couldn't say no to Queen.

That night Franks dropped the mic'. His voice was a dolce tone, actually musical and deep. Before, panties were dropping like anvils from a plane, now, after Franks did Keith Urban's "Blue Ain't Your Color", those same knickers were going up in flame; spontaneous combustion. Faces were being fanned. Checks turning red. And even a couple of male trousers becoming uncomfortably snug.

Franks stayed until Penny, Nick and Andy left.

"Franks, see you next week. Naw, Nick's car is parked by our house. We'll give him a ride. NO! I mean, naw, you don't need to come. No need at all."

Out the door they went. A few minutes later, one last pitcher for the walk home, Franks exited the place and started to make his way north. His apartment was a couple of miles away, but the night air was cool, and, after sitting down for so long on a stool, he could use the exercise. 2 block, 6 blocks, a mile and he kept going.

Beam-lights spotted him less than a few yards from his house. He turned and cupped his hands over his eyes. A car started to slow down. It made its way next to Franks, lowered its window and he heard a voice he instantly recognized.

"Hey, need a lift?" Inside, Jeanne, Andy's little sister unlocked the door. There was something odd. Something out of place. Her mouth was inviting him, her voice seducing him in, but her eyes told another tale. They were afraid. Something wasn't kosher. Franks had noticed Jeanne in the bar. Cute, not exactly a femme fatale but cute. Small and pixie like. A Tinkerbell really. A cute bubble butt supported by two shapely legs. The front had a pair of breasts that were a bit too large and disproportionate to the whole ensemble. Then there was the hair. All the times Franks had met Jeanne, she always had her auburn locks tied up in a practical pony tail. Not any more. Now, she had dyed her mane a flashy ruby red and tossed out practicality for a savage look; frizzy, like she had just woken up after a wild night. Still, there was something off about the whole thing.

"He going to come in?" A voice asked from the back seat. He recognized it.

Frank peered in, "what the fuck!"

What could only be described as very out off whack, off her medicine, Scarlett Johansson, pressed the barrel of a .44 to the back of Jeanne's seat.

"Hey, Franks," the bat shit crazy, off her rocker loon said, "been a while." She cocked back the trigger.

"Son of bitch. Moira, not this shit again."

"Get in the car, Franks."

"You know this crazy bitch?" Andy's sister asked. "Was getting in my car when she jumped me. Had me driving around the neighborhood 'till she spotted you."

"Jeanne," Franks opened the backdoor and slid inside, "meet Moira, my ex…"

"What we had was amazing. Life altering."

"We had a fling," Franks sat down.

"I can't get you out of my mind."

"Moira?" Went Jeanne. "That name rings a bell."

"Co-worker of Penny. Just got married a year ago…"

"I'm pregnant with your kid," Moira exclaimed.

"Total fruitcake," goes Franks.

"Didn't you hear me?" Moira pushed the gun further into the back of the seat, the muzzle buried deep into the upholstery. "Franks, you're going to be a dad. I'll divorce Rick and we can start a family. Do it right this time. If not for me, then for Tommy."

"You already named the kid?" Asked a quaking Jeanne.

"Tommy, like the Who album. First time Franks and me made love was to the sound of The Pinball Wizard… Franks, you have to do the responsible thing. Your seed is growing in my belly."

"Jesus on a moped," Franks sighed. "The last time we had sex was 2 years ago. Unless it's a mutant, I doubt it's my kid. Moira, go back to Rick and give him the good news. Drop the fucking gun and we'll call it another one of your panic attacks."

"Two years?" Went Jeanne. "What a basketcase."

"It's your's Franks… I can feel it."

"I feel like this is a tired troupe," went Jeanne.

"Once every few months. She's medicated, she just forgets to take her pills every once in a while." Franks said nonchalantly. "Leave it to me."

"What do you want Moira?" Frank asked.

"I want you Frank. I want you."

"Man, what the fuck did you do to her?" Jeanne asked.

"Take me to your apartment," a gun pressed into the back of the seat once more. "Your apartment, NOW."

"Not going to happen," two ham sized arms crossed themselves.

"Not even if you were holding a bazooka."

"Really?" Shaking in her seat Jeanne went.

"Give this looney tunes my address? I might as well swallow arsenic."

"Frank," Moira's hand went down and grabbed hold of his groin, "you know how this ends."

"I don't," Jeanne said.

"She wants me to fuck her," Franks huffed.

"What?!"

"I need you Franks. I need that," a crazy woman's fingers dug deep into his thigh.

"My apartments is just around the corner?" Went Jeanne.

"Oh fuck," Frank glowered.

A voice, the sort that comes out of a phone when calling a hot line - if said hot line was being maned by escapes from an insane asylum - yipped: "move…" That's the second everything went to hell in a hand basket.

20 minutes later, Franks was tied spread eagle on a mattress. Moira having brought to the kidnapping party not just a handgun.

"Parachord. Moira, of all the things I thought you why did that one have to stick?"

Jeanne on top of Franks tightening the nooses, a gun pointed at her from across the room. "I'm really sorry."

Moira, meanwhile, was smoking a cigarette and trying her best not to burn her breast with the falling ashes. Her clothes tossed in a heap. The minute she skated into the room, she realized that she was over-dressed; crazy, it seemed, was like menopause, full of hot flashes.

"Cut his clothes off," commanded the throw-away gag of a very badly written exploitation film. "All of them."

Jeanne went to her dresser and started rummaging: "I only have nail clippers…"

"Jesus, sister, is this your first kidnapping?… For god's sake go and get a kitchen knife."

"I really liked that shirt," Franks went minutes afterwards.

"I'm really, really sorry," Jeanne using a pair of garden sheers once Franks pointed out that her chef's knife was in need of a good sharpening. She traced the scissors down the side of his legs and shredded his jeans off. Jeanne marveled at his strong legs, each like an oil barrel, and was fast becoming dizzy with his aroma. She was scared shitless, but a part of her, one that hand't gotten the message saying that they were in a slasher movie, was screaming at her and demanding some nookie. Franks shirt was off. Jeanne had seen hundreds of men, most in adds and the screen. Hundreds of guys that looked like they slept in the gym. Underwear models who no doubt ate nothing but protein and ran a half a marathon on a daily basis. Dozens of would be action stars, like Jason Statham - her favorite - that oozed testosterone. Crowds of disposable muscle heads and steroid addicts that pranced around the nigh clubs she visited like they were the kings of the place. None, not a single one of them, could hold a candle to Frank's physique.

She gulped and asked, "you want me to cut his boxers off?"
Then, while she was twitching with anticipation, a hand came from behind. She felt a piece of fabric against her mouth and nose. An ether like odor ran up her nostrils, a sweet taste clung to her throat. Her eyes went numb, everything went dark.

"What the…" Jeanne started to orient herself. A hand was slapping her cheeks. She looked up and, sure enough, there was Moira. The statuesque nutball completely naked and straddling her bare chest; knees clamped around her knees. Jeanne struggled, ropes bit into her wrist; she looked down. "We are my clothes?!"
"Manic Depressive Rainbow Pony stripped you and bound you up," Franks said besides her.
"Love the fact that you have two beds in this room," Moira said. "let me guess, used to have a roommate?"
Jeanne wanted to scream but her throat still ached.
"It's the chloroform. Her purse is like Santa's bag," went Franks. Moira slid off Jeanne, and without missing a crazy beat, sat besides Franks and started stroking his cock. Jeanne was half asleep, so she most have been dreaming, because the thing Franks was sporting looked like a huge crossbeam; the guy had a third leg… one as meaty and well formed as the others.
Moira caught Jeanne's look, "and it's not even hard. Wait 'till it's erect. It's like the Eiffel Tower." Then, as if time was going to expire and they needed to speed thing up, Moira bend down and

started giving Franks a blowjob. Up and down she went on the huge shaft. She could hardly fit a third of it; her mouth unhinging like one of those anacondas they're so fond of showing on The Discovery Channel. She was gagging on the thickest cock Jeanne had ever seen. "And it's not even hard," she recalled.

Moira got up, took a breath, "I felt it grow… See, Franks, you do love me."

"It's not love, it's my lizard brain fucking with me."

Moira, "I know what will get your Gibraltar ready for me."

She got up, and before Jeanne could protest, crazy brains dipped between her legs and started doings things to her pussy. She began playing with her clit, and despite the fact that it was forced, despite the fact that it was humiliating, despite the fact that she wanted to scream, all she could do was moan the second Moira's nose flicked her bell. She pulled against the ropes, not to free herself but to give free reign to the tension and electricity flowing up her body. Moira's tongue found her clit, first the tip, then the whole thing. Jeanne explored in ecstasy and Moira took it as a sign. The basket case put her whole mouth over her captive's opening and made an airless seal. It was incredible, like nothing she had ever felt before. She wriggled as lips played with lips, hot breath warmed her skin, a wanton mouth engulfed her whole. She turned and saw Franks, their eyes meet, she looked down and saw that Moira was having a lasting effect on the big guy. Looney Tunes was right, "**Wait 'till it's erect.**"

Jeanne came the second she realized that the Paris landmark looked dwarfish next to Frank's powerful monster. She shuttered with involuntary spasms, Moira's very apt and incredibly nimble mouth doing things to her that few, and maybe none, had done.

"It's always the crazy ones," Frank said. "Something about their abhorrent genetic makes them bombastic in the sack. Moira's a firecracker and this girl I once dated, a Satanist, could make you renounce Jesus just by looking at you."

Jeanne was still riding Moira's tongue, or more to the point, Moira was riding her body while Franks pontificated. The psycho made her break every crest and surf along a sea of pleasure. When she couldn't take it any more, when her wriggles and struggles were making the chords dig her wrist and cut her circulation, when she was seconds from passing out, when the pain of her restriction was too unbearable, only then did Moira stop. Moira looked up from between Jeanne's legs, like a groundhog foretelling how long winter would last, and smiled.

"A girl can have great tits. She had can a fantastic body. She can look like a supermodel and have legs that climb up to her ears, but if she doesn't taste good, if her lips aren't yummy, she's a zero in my book," Moira climbed unto Jeanne's belly, sat over her rip cage. "And cutie, you're a 10," trailing a finger back down Jeanne's cunt and then licking it clean, "In my book." Moira then pressed against Jeanne's belly button and let the juices from her moist vagina run down the side of her captive's shivering body.

Jeanne was gasping, fear and the adrenaline of the assault, amping the sex; making the whole whirlwind into an epic scenario. The thumb of her heart pumping mad in her chest, as she stared at the crazy bimbo getting off her now damp naked body and gearing to ride Franks like a rodeo bull, beat inside her ear drums and made her have hot flashes. Was she climaxing again? She was. She was definitely having micro-orgasms.

Moira grabbed Franks by the throat and lowered her whole body onto his massive tool. Jeanne saw her bit down on her lower lip, the shock of Frank's bulge testing the limits of a vagina's elasticity. Moira dug her fingernails into Franks shoulder, screaming with a mix of pain, dread and exhilaration as she stabbed herself, all the way to hilt, with Frank. It looked like it really hurt. It looked like he was tearing her in half, while in fact being raped by her. It looked like Moira's wraith like body, slick, tall and muscular, was barely able to contain Frank's. It looked like, if the shoe was on the other foot, and it was Jeanne doing the fucking, her pixie like body, small and petite, would bleed under Frank's powerful anatomy. Moira rode Frank and shouted encouragement. She shouted every sexual invective in the book. She shouted things that would have seemed hardcore even in a porn movie. She was rapping him, closing off his windpipe and making him partly pass-out whenever he was about to climax, while also being almost ripped in two. Jeanne, was now certain, that Franks would have made her bleed… and as her pussy started to throb, she realized that sometime a little blood is just what the doctor ordered.

Jeanne didn't know it but she was allowing her arousal to become vocal, she was giving off small squeals of delight. Moira, riding Franks, breast pendulum in every direction, hair caught in a self-made hurricane, snatched the small cries. Without peeling her eyes off of Franks, Moira brought down her hand and smacked Jeanne across the face. Then, just so she could disorient her captive a bit more - there's nothing in the world more vexing than giving off mixed signals in a hostage, or in any situation at that - Moira reached between Jeanne's legs and started to masturbate her.

Jeanne wriggled against her bonds. She pulled at them. She cursed. She crossed her legs. She bled from her wrist. Moira didn't give a fuck. "Stop… Stop… Please stop…"

Frank was buckling under the goth princess' ride 'em cowboy phase. "Oh, god… Oh, god… oh, god."

Jeanne saw Frank's eyes turn up in his skull, the whites now occupying the whole occipital orbit. He groaned and tossed his pelvis up, Moira hung on for dear life, "yes, yes, yes, yes, yes…"

Jeanne felt another orgasm coming, she licked her lips, spat out in defense, wrestled against her worst demons, but the second she saw that Frank's was cumming and Moira's insides were getting doused, she could hold back. She pushed against Moira's fingers, hopping that one would penetrate her, hopping that somehow that little digit could like the three of them together. That she could feel Frank's throbbing cock through it. Moira, the ever diligent pervert and screw loose, obliged. She aimed for Jeanne's G-spot and her aim was true. Moira fell back against Frank's curling toes, Jeanne kept wriggling against the invading digit, Franks just sighed. The big man resigned to the ignominy of being hogtied and manhandled by a fruit loose like Moira…well, partly resigned, he was still a guy. For the first time that night he actually took a couple of moments to get a gander of Andy's sister. The girl, Frank's declared inwardly, was alright. As far as sexual thumbs up, that in Frank's vocabulary was akin to a cartoon wolf going apeshit at the sight of a hot nurse; eyes bulging out of their sockets, 3 times the size of the lupine's head, out falling open and a tongue unrolling.

Moira decide to up the ante, in for for penny and all that claptrap. Her hubby was a marvel in the sack, the fella' an insatiable monster who simply couldn't get enough of her candy. He'd come home, and right after shutting the door, he'd jump out of his pants and come at her with an erection that would have been the envy of many women. She had, for all intents and purposes, and ideal marriage. A great looking, loaded with dough, fun as hell husband with the sex-drive of a horny teenager. She stared at Frank's barrel chest and all ready hard cock. Yeah, she had a husband most dames would have sold their souls for… But he sure as hell wasn't Franks. Franks could get under your skin, like some toxic mold or fatal virus, and once you caught it, once you had it, penicillin and anti-virus just barely managed keep the symptoms tamped down; the infection never left you. Moira got on her knees, with one hand she started cupping and massaging Frank's testicles, with the other she penetrated herself, going deep. One finger, then two, then three, all the way up to the knuckles. The virus never went away, and every-so-often, it would flare up.

Jeanne looked at Moira, the crazy bitch having what could only be described as an out-of-body experience. Franks in less than two minutes was once more at full mast. "Christ," Jeanne told no-one in particular, "his dick is still wet with cum." She, her body once more taking a bat to her sanity, started to get moist. The view of Frank's oak like shaft, shinning wet with a blend of semen and Moira's juices, was making her thoughts runaway with all semblance of logic. Here she was, tied up, scared shitless, the gun she had been cowed with less than a meter away on her night stand, a hostage of a very perturbed woman, for all intents and purpose a rape victim, wiggling with delight and praying for the night to continue. Stockholm Syndrome, in Jeanne's case, came in fast and wearing a see through gown.

Before Jeanne could wrap her head around what was happening, Moira, in sheer abandon, and with the speed of a puma, jumped on her face and started smothering her. Moira pressed her pussy against Jeanne's mouth, two fingers parting the lips and forcing the salty clit against her tongue. Jeanne could barely breath, she couldn't control the force. On instinct, not experience, Jeanne went with the flow.

"Franks, you like this?" Moira went. "I can tell she's never done this. You should feel her tongue down there, amateur hour." Moira started grinding against her victim's mouth, a she grabbed Jeanne's dyed hair and forced her against her opening; seizing the wheel and controlling the pace. She started to moan, touching her breast, and pinching her nipples. In bouts of pleasure and delight, she raked her nails across Frank's chest.

Jeanne, lapped her kidnapper's cunt like a kitty with a bowl of milk. She couldn't help herself, she could feel Moira's heartbeat against her lips, she could taste her - a bittersweet mix of salt with vanilla. Jeanne could feel, coming down into her throat, skidding across the insides of her cheeks, Frank's semen; still hot. Moira was riding her like a horse through a prairie. Then, she felt opportunity knocking. The knots on her left arms were being untied.

Jeanne glimpse sideways and saw, to her astonishment, that Moira was cracking her chains open. Then, the nutcase went for her right. She flexed, circulation coming back to her hands. She was partly free, her legs still tied and spread, but her hands and arms back in the game. Moira put both her hands on top of Jeanne's head, held her firm against the mattress and pressed her vagina harder, like her life depended on it, against a tongue that simply couldn't stop itself. Jeanne's hands came up, they went to the psycho's neck and wrapped themselves around a dandy windpipe. A thumb pressed hard, Moira started heave and cough. Jeanne squeezed, Moira started to flay. Jeanne gripped and cut in her nails, she felt blood running down one finger. She was choking Moira, and still the crazy nutball wouldn't quit pressing her pussy against her... her delicious wet, cum filled pussy. The same pussy Jeanne couldn't stop licking. Before she knew it, Jeanne let go of Moira's throat. Hands falling down a sweaty back. Fingers skipping along a spinal column, trailing tattoos, and pickling sensations into life. Moira, pressed against Jeanne once more, she started to slide up and down; marking a river of fluids from her mouth down to her clavicle. Butt checks glanced against erect nipples and made jolts of electricity travel from Jeanne's chest all the way down to her vagina. Jeanne's hands grabbed hold of Moira's tight - I bet she goes to spin class - behind and pushed her back into place; back where she belonged. She demanded that Moira keep on face fucking her.

Then, Moira, minutes from once more climaxing, felt Jeanne's vengeance. It came from behind, no preamble, no warning, just a force of nature battering in. She felt fingers part her asscheeks and penetrate her. It was rough, it was angry, it was pissed. It was all the pent up frustration of Jeanne, all her wrath and distain at was happening bottled and canalized in violent fashion. She was being impaled, up to the wrist, by Jeanne's revenge. Moira came like she had never come before.

Frank's saw the scene, and said: "I've seen the trailer for this film before."

Moira was laying exhausted over Jeanne. Jeanne, meanwhile, was pushing the lifeless doll out of the way; she wasn't carving any headway… Moira was deadweight. Franks knew what was coming next. He wanted to say, "not this shit again."

Moira, roused herself back to life, flung her legs from the sides of Jeanne's head and went in for a kiss. This was the moment when all cards for the future of the game would be dealt. Moira put her lips over Jeanne's and started to passionately devour her… Jeanne, responded back with the same fervor.

The crazy chicks were like fine dope to a recovering addict. Moira and Jeanne started to make out next to Franks. Franks knew what would happen next, he knew that the night had just begun. Franks hoped that Moira, and now Jeanne, would never notice that the Parachord had somehow gotten loose and that his left arm wasn't tied up. It had never really been tightly fixed. Franks knew, above everything else, how to play the game… Otherwise, he would have made a big deal, screaming his head off, when Moira shoved the .44 against Jeanne's back… He would have laughed his ass off at the fact that the black paint was dripping down the muzzle, the plastic red of a water gun visible. Franks would have pointed it out, but he didn't. Yup, Franks knew how to play the game, and the number one rule is: enjoy the ride.

DREAMS OF CALIFORNICATION

"That night, by the pool had been a game changer. Moira and Amanda not only rocked my world but quite possible blew it up. What I didn't identify, until years later, was that it hadn't really changed the game so much as finished it. In the way, that was the year I peaked. My life slowly transformed into a by the numbers rendition of a Bruce Springsteen song. Reality started handing me lemons and I wasn't mature or smart enough to add sugar and make lemonade.

It took Moira less than 24 hours after that sexually charged night to turn into a full-blown possessive psycho. She could have given Glen Close stalking tips; if I even though about getting close to Amanda she went gonzo. I swear, she basically branded Amanda's ass with her name. Looking at my stepsister, with just a glint of lust, instantly got Moira on my bad side… and the least I could expect from that crazy 'puta' was a dead bunny.

Then, just like that weekend had been a eye opener for me, it also seemed to wash away the pixie dust from Amanda's mom eyes. God only knows what happened in Cancun but the minute my dad and her walked into the house after their trip you instantly understood that the marriage had finally soured. Amanda's mom was a frigid icecap; each time she entered the room, and my dad was there, the ambient temperature would dip about 40 degrees. In a month we were out on our asses. A pre-nup, a good lawyer and enough evidence of his cheating ways ended up paving my dad's road back to the part of town middle America likes to avoid… and he dragged me along for the ride.

Then came blow after blow. No more pools. No swim-meets. No nice school. No insurance. No nothing. We had jack-shit and were creating debts left and right. Paying a daily rate at a Days Inn that had been overtaken by hookers, drug dealers, welfare families and tourist who had never heard of TripAdvisor. My love life, meanwhile, was kicked in the balls. You're hot latin shit when your striding around in what can only be described as privileged white academy, but in the ghetto you're just another tanned clone that crackers come up to and ask: 'you mexican?' 'No.' 'O.K, than that's alright.'… gangs trying to figure out if you're spick, a vato, or something else. Head down and doing your best not call any attention.

One day, I come back from school. Not even a note just a ball of 20s crumbled next to the TV; 460 dollars supplanting my old man's stuff. The shelves were bare, his suitcase gone. The father unit didn't event have the decency to claim that he was going out for cigs'. I dropped out of high school a week later. Needed to round up the scratch, otherwise I was on my ass… Plus, I was still a minor. If the big dogs got wind that I was flying solo I'd be shipped off into the system. I started doing odd jobs around the Days Inn. Some for the manager, they had a rotating door of employees that simply didn't cut it; hosing drunks off the picnic area by the pool, while dodging beer cans really took the sheen off minimum wage. Some of the other jobs were for the long stay residents; taking their brats to school, helping them with an odd job or two. And some of the work… well… it was for the sketchy remora entrepreneurs that made the motel their base of operations.

A good day was when I made 30 buck, 29 plus tax was the room rate. A great day was when a made a bit more and I had enough for a 7-11 value meal. There were more bad days than good; half the time I was sleeping in the box stop and dumpster diving.

Then, one afternoon the whole thing changed. Life was still giving me lemons, only this time it added an extra ingredient; spicy caribbean rum. 'I'll give you 50 bucks to eat out my wife.' One of the theme park tourists wanted something a bit more risqué than Space Mountain it seemed. Guy simply called me up to his hotel room and told me flat; no preamble, nothing. Life didn't want me to make lemonades, it wanted me to mix up a batch of mojitos. I didn't have to be told twice. My swimmer's body had gone the way of the dodo, but my lack of a daily meal compensated. I was less muscular, more fiber, but I could still turn heads. I went into a room and prayed she had all her teeth. The snatch in question was a nice looking 46 year old; the type called a MILF. Two for two I thought. I earned my 50 bucks in record time. Her husband sitting next to us in bed, completely naked, stroking his cock while his wife moaned. When I had made her cum, he pushed me aside, penetrated her wet pussy and in less than 15 seconds dumped his load next to mine. I didn't have any Trojans and in hindsight I realized that we were all playing Russian Roulette.

'An extra 20,' he huffed, 'if you clean her out.'

I really did need the cash. Didn't even catch their name afterwards. The MILF never said a goddamn word. She had been silent as a statue the whole time. Not even a squeal.

It sort of became a regular thing. Once a week, they'd come by, he'd slip me a 50 and I'd go up and pleasure his wife. Sometimes I'd take my cloths off, other times I'd leave them on. Then, if the mood called for it, he'd give me that 20 extra tip with that rather bizarre clause. For 3 months his old lady didn't say a thing. When she finally did, mid oral fest, it ended up earning me enough to go the Ponderosa that evening. 'Nate… I want him to fuck me… I want that cock…'

Nate, and I later found out, Gilda, lived a couple of miles up the road. Full blown suburban bliss. They weren't tourist but residents. Good house, great neighborhood, P.T.A. on Wednesday, one kid about to enter an ivy league, the other a tract star and daughter in pre-med, a border collie and white picket fences.

'Juan,' one day all us drenched and dehydrated on the filthy mattress, Nate went, 'you mind if we pass your contact along?' And that's how I discovered what a 'bull' was. I had a new profession.

I started fucking desperate housewives, horny sorority girls looking for a thrill, and jilted lovers almost every night. My rates went up when I got a gym membership. I rented a nice looking AirBnb, a week in I went back to the flea-bag motel… part of the turn on, it seemed, was the seedy scenery.

I'd drilled doggy-style while a willing husband would lube up a backdoor entrance and growl: 'now do her there.' I'd stand in front of a mirror, I bought a full length one, while a naughty school teacher would kneel completely naked and give me a blowjob, one hand on her boyfriend's erect penis. 'Cum on my face. Cum all over it,' then she'd switch; hot raw hand on my shaft, lubricated with pre-ejaculate and her spit, wet lips on his.

'Oh god, it feels so different… God, I love you,' lesbian lovers from Montana. The 'I love you part' directed not at me but at her partner. Tear flowing down a face.

'She's never had a man,' a 32-year-old crew-cut blond told me while sitting on a freckled face; a clit grinding against an eager mouth.

'You want me to slow down?'

'No… fuck her harder… It's her birthday gift,' then she pulled me in and made me suck her nipples; one of them pierced with a gold ring.

Everyone, I found out in my three years of working the beat, had a weird fetish. Housewives who had read too much 50 Shades Of Grey and now wanted to get spanked raw; their old man off in the

office unaware of that particular taste. Girls barely out of high school that wanted to be man handled, shirts ripped from their bodies, and choked. Men who wanted to be tied up, their dicks placed in a small cage and verbally humiliated while their wife's were getting fucked by me. 'Harry, now that's a fucking cock… God, it feel so good. It's so big. I God, I've never come so good. Harder. Harder. He's going to cum all inside of me. Probably fill me up 'till I burst with his hot load. And what are you going to do about it you limp dick asshole?'
'Clean you up, my love…'
'That's right… Harder… You really are a little boy.'
The Big fantasies were:
'Brat Play': 'but It's so big. No, you can make me suck you off. You can't. It's too big, daddy. I don't thing I'll be able to fit it in… Stop it. Stop it. Don't rip off my panties.' Mind you, most of them came to my door wearing stockings, Converse sneakers, a tight Hello Kitty shirt and sucking on a lollypop.
'Rape simulation': which, after getting asked to do a breaking and entry on a house with a toy gun, now required a signed consent form; notarized at that.
And 'male-female-male threesome,' you really can't imagine how many men want to see their wife or girlfriend being fucked. Nor can you imagine how many of them, after degrading their loved ones, start to get frisky with my tool.
'It's still hard…'

'God,' legs spread open, pussy still drenching with her husband's cum, 'I want you to suck him off. I want to see that.' If I had a buck for every time a threesome turned into a male experimentation session I'd most likely have a enough for a down payment on a Condo.

Once, I still remember, this restaurant manager calls me up and tells me. 'I think I'm bisexual.' Next day, he's in the hotel room, his ass cheeks spread and I'm coming in hot. I'm giving him a proper fucking when the door burst open and in comes a screaming banshee. It's his wife. She's in tears, pissed off and screaming all over the place. 'You fucking homo,' she says. 'God, what I'm I going to tell the kids?' She says. 'You better be fucking with protection,' she says. 'I'm so going to divorce you,' she says and takes a couple of pictures. Meanwhile, I want to get out of that clusterfuck and run for the hills, but the guy isn't even slowing down. He's getting berated by the mother of their children and he won't even stop; he's pushing against my dick, making me drill him hard, moaning all the while.

'Stop doing that! It's disgusting…' He doesn't. He keeps going at it.

'Stop it,' then a full 180, 'it's turning me on.'

She lays on the bed, takes off her pants and starts masturbating. Every-so-often, still pissed and crying, she'd take a swing at her husband and slap him across the face.

'I really should stop,' I go.

'No,' both of them go.

'I want you to stroke his cock, but not make him cum.' She tells me. 'And I want you to tell me when you're about to climax.' Her husband close mouth and not saying a word.

20 minutes later, I'm pulling out, per her orders, and she's taking off my condom and making me cum all over her husband's face. Then, because she's still crying, sayin' that we destroyed a household, sayin' 'you're a home-wrecker,' I end up fucking her while she's slapping her husband black and blue. 2 hours later, they're out the door, both steaming like crazy. I don't vent get payed.

'The Johnsons,' goes a friend who is also in the business.

'You know them?'

'Yeah. How did you think she found out which room and which hotel you were staying at? Hell, for that matter, didn't you close the door? Let me guess the husband came in last. Count yourself lucky, with me she brought accessories. You have no idea how creative that bitch can get with what's ever handy in her purse.'

After a while, that sort of thing - getting jibbed - becomes a hazard of the job. I stayed in that La La Land, my own private amusement ride, for couples until I was 23. By that time I had done absolutely everything and for that matter been submitted to a great deal more. Things that would rattle the sanest imagination.

I had gone to a Furry convention, and been treated to a one hour lecture on the difference between a furry and a yiff… Then I got the once in a lifetime chance to fuck a Unicorn up the ass.

I had been taken, all expenses paid, to the Bahamas as a boy toy for a married couple. Best of all, the man had charged me with the mission to fetch him a lady of night to join us. I had contacts and for what they were paying and offering up as benefits I had my pick of the litter. That week we did it all around town. Best spot? On the villa's balcony, the young girl I'd brought, legs spread, gripped to the railing while I plunged deep; the sun sinking in the ocean.

I went to a weddings as a plus one and got the chance to do the bride, per her husband's instructions, minutes before the ceremony. The virginal lady completely naked, the gown - less you flick bad luck in the eye - in a closet out off sight. The soon to be cock-old making her swallow my cum. 'Don't you dare wash your mouth.' On the altar, 'you may now kiss the bride,' two mouths pressed against each other… I got a hard-on seeing the scene and knowing that I was still on her lips. That night, I was invited into the wedding suite; she never once took off her dress.

There were insane things that boggled the mind. 'I'm not putting cocaine on my cock!'

There were bizarre hiccups along the way. 'Buddy, you have the wrong house.' In the back a wife frantically moving her arms in a no-no gesture out of her hubby's eye line.

On my 23rd year ,I packed up, needing a change of scenery and bought, as the Boss, sang 'two tickets on that Coast City bus.' I headed to L.A. Stopping along the way and a doing some carnal sightseeing; Southern Girls are the best.

By the time I reached L.A. I had more sexual experience than most porn actors twice my age… The Hollywood hills instantly got wind and before long I was making 3 to 4 thousand bucks for a 3 hour shot.

I re-meet Amanda a couple of years later, but that's a story for another time…"

WORKIN' 9 TO 5, WHAT A WAY TO MAKE A LIVIN'

"Shit," Amanda said under her breath. She flung into the office supply closet and hoped she hadn't been spotted. Out the door, from crack she could spy from, she made a cautionary inspection. It had been a close call. Amanda had been doing her level best to avoid Moira at work.
Moira had been her best friend back in the heydays of High School. She was the sort of buddy you just knew was bad for your health. When parents around the world said "they are a bad influence" or "your running with the wrong crowd", they might as well have been talking about Moira. Moira was bad on a scale of a cataclysm. She was bad and toxic in the way Chernobyl was radioactive. She was the sort of girl, potheads, dope fiends and serial killers would give a wide berth to… And, back in High School, Moira was catnip to someone like Amanda. She was suicide by friendship. If you wanted to rebel, if you wanted to go against the system, or if you simply wanted to cause a fuzz because mommy and daddy split up, then Moira was the nuclear option. Moira was the perfect temple tantrum.

Moira was up for anything. Illegal, immoral, batshit crazy, she didn't care.

Back in High School, Moira had been a blast. To Amanda she was that one girl all girls should aspire to. Fearless. Engaging. Charming. Wild. From a good family that galvanized their child to express themselves. Moira was a fire-craker. Amanda had developed a crush on Moira right out of the gate. Moira took her to get her first and only tattoo. Moira thought her how to smoke. Moira thought her how to score weed. Moira thought her how to kiss. And, Moira, well, Moira had been her first. Moira had made her climax like no other boy her age could have.

"Just let me in… trust me, you'll like it," Moira had said. Amanda was partly baked so she wasn't exactly putting up a fight. Moira went down on her and, as it turned out, it was a one way street.

"And this is a how you give a blowjob," Moira had gone days after making Amanda have her first orgasms. Both of them were naked in Moira's room, Amanda still soaked in sweat and licking her lips, Moira's juices just now drying up. "You have to grab the balls, and then…" Moira swallowed the plastic shaft of a black dildo until she was gagging; rivulets of frothing spit coming off it and hitting the floor. That day Amanda learned how to get facefucked, she also lost her virginity… a black dildo pushing pass her hymen as Moira kissed her tears away. "It'll only hurt for a minute."

Moira had been the girl who taught her absolutely everything in life; especially everything sexually. With Moira, Amanda had tried her first threesome - and maybe, in hindsight, even participated in a bit of incest. She wasn't sure what rules were about fucking your stepbrother.

"Are black cocks really that great?" Amanda had asked Moira on day. Moira stumped, not something that happened to THE teacher, responded a week later. It turns out you can find anything on Ebay. His name was Omar, and although he charged by the hour, he decided to wage his fee the minute Moira told him to fuck me in the ass.

Moira was an astroid strike. Then, weeks after graduation, Amanda realized that Moira, just like an asteroid strike, was also, by her very nature, an extinction level event.

Things started to spiral out of control. Moira's jealousy reached new levels of persecution. She started to follow Amanda all over town. She had Amanda's phone bugged. She had every thing about Amanda tapped.

"Hey, I got accepted to NYU!"

"The fuck you're going to New York!"

Then, one day, Moira just disappeared. Puff, like a magician that had out stayed his welcome. Amanda went to college, got a degree in Business and Finances and moved back home. In the Big Apple she was just a small fish in an ocean of sharks. Back home, in the pond they called their town, she was hot shit; she was the shark. She was instantly swooped up into a Multi national that traded in bonds and foreign debt from other countries. She became a jet-setter, traveling to Brazil, Argentina, Uruguay, Korea, Bangladesh, putting out fires and telling the big boys where to invest.

By the time Amanda was 34, she had her life squared and tied up in bow. Everything was working out to perfection. Well, almost everything, her professional workload had put a fritz on her love-life. She was hot. She was blond. She was statuesque. She ran marathons in her spare time. She could benchpress 100 kilos. She had the skin of a 20 year-old. Plus, due to her runner's build, she had a silicone job that was the envy of everyone of her co-workers. Amanda could have any man or woman on the planet… yet somehow all she really manage to score were inordinate amounts of double D batteries; her vibrator collection getting worrisome.

And, because fate has a nasty sense of humor, at her most vulnerable, a knock came to her door.

"Moira?"

That night, and almost a month afterwards, Moira as sexy as ever and with more tattoos than before, rocked Amanda's world. In her 12 years of absence, "been all over the place", Moira had learned things.

"It's called the Venus Butterfly."

"Tantra, Amanda, don't come yet… This is how you become multi-orgasmic."

"It's like Spanish Fly only real."

"Bough it in Singapore. It's illegal in the states. Why? Something about its motor being too powerful."

And that is how, 3 weeks in, Moira got a job at Amanda's office; the mother of all faux-passes.

Two years later, Amanda was hiding in the closet, seeing the screw loose of her friend skate down the corridor. Moira had somehow married a junior executive. A guy most of the girls were gonzo about. Amanda, on their wedding day, had basically danced a jig and counted her lucky stars; the crazy bitch was emotionally out of her life. "Hurray!"

Then the erotic texts came… followed by the photos. "Did she use a selfistick for that angle?"… and the calls at 3 in the morning… And Moira's hand brushing her backside at work. It was sexual harassment, if not for the fact that Moira was her junior and Amanda wasn't exactly a choir girl. What a clusterfuck.

"You hiding from someone?" Amanda screeched and turned back into the closet.

Seating on a box of packed folders, eating out off a Tupperware, a man chewed.

"James, what the fuck are you doing in here?"

"Lunch break."

"It's 3 in the afternoon?"

"Yeah, used my lunch break to goof around… Didn't have anything to eat… Told my boss I was going to get some critical paperwork from storage… and here I am… that was," looking at his watch, "about 30 minutes ago."

"James, you do know I'm your boss' boss?"

"You going to snitch me out?" A grin. "Got some M&ms if you're egging for a bribe."

Moira was coming back down the corridor.

Amanda, slowly, closed the door, "peanut or milk chocolate?"

"Better, Peanut Butter."

"The food of the Gods," Amanda said as she sat down next to James.

They never went back to work that day. James was the well mannered dork, a spitting image of David Tennant from Doctor Who, that Amanda could never get aroused with… Yet, here in the almost dark of the supply closet, James clumsily hitting on her, she discovered the benefits of a healthy relationship. He was funny, and in a rather bizarre way he really was sexy; in the way David Bowie or Tilda Swinton were sexy. James had androgynous features that drove her wild.

"Your bi, right?" Amanda blurted out. "Shit, don't report me to H.R."

"You didn't snitch, so you get a pass. Is it that obvious? Is it the look?"

"No, radar sense," Amanda pointed at herself. "It takes one to no one."

Then, the Moonage Daydream made a not so subtle pass. James took off his shoes and slowly traced Amanda's long legs. His toes sliding up a black lycra stockings. His heel pointed upwards, his foot going inside her skirt. Amanda stopped his foot just at the ankle. The footloose fella' was inches away from her panties.

"What. The. Fuck. Do. You. Think. You're. Doing?"

A deer caught in the headlights. James gulped and started to stammer. Amanda lounged for him. Weeks of pent up sexual frustration erupting in a supply closet. Limps went everywhere; arms outstretched. Fabric flew around the place. Bite marks appeared out of nowhere. It was a sexual encounter by way of the Tasmanian Devil; a dervish cloud where outsiders could only guess what was happening.

10 minutes later, boxes crunched under body parts, pencils thrown nilly dilly about, a copy machine's toner cracked open, "you have some ink on your hair, Amanda," two bodies huffed in a heated exhaustion.

"Well, you really liked those M&ms… I have to take you to the retail store."

"Shut up, you dork," Amanda inspecting her stockings and realizing that they were a lost cause. She slit what was left into a side pocket of her jacket. "Come on, zip me up."

James, naked from the waist down, came up to Amanda's back and started to untangle hair from a rather fidgety zipper. "You want to do something later on? Maybe hit a club."

"James, you're sweet… Are you still hard?" Amanda felt something poke her thigh.

"Always…"

"As I said, you're sweet. But this is a one time thing…"

Three weeks later, Amanda had no choice but to swallow her pride and accept Jame's invitation. It was the least she could do. After all, the Harry Potter enthusiast had kept his mouth shut. He hadn't blabbed to a single person about what went down in the supply closet that afternoon… Or what happened on the conference table two days afterwards. "James, you can't moan… I'm having a telephone conference," a finger flicking mute off. "Sorry about that, one of my staff members had something stuck in his throat." James didn't say a single thing about that afternoon as he let Amanda ride him on a chair… Or about the time it was raining and they casually met in the parking lot. "Damn, Amanda, where the hell did you learn to suck like that?" Not one word… Or about the time he hid under Amanda's desk and licked her until she came, the blinds of her office partly open, everybody in the bullpen oblivious to the fact that she had her panties around Jame's neck. Not even a pip… Or, well, the other 12 or so times she'd call him on her extension for an urgent meeting or he's stumble onto her path as they entered the elevator. "This has to stop, there are cameras up there. How do you know there's no one watching them? You have to stop finger fucking me in here… It's not safe…Oh, God. Never mind, don't stop."

"So," went Amanda dressed to the nines, "this is a trans bar?"
"An LGBT friendly bar… but yeah, a tranny bar."

A girl? Or was it a boy? Flashed past Amanda. Her eyes almost fell out of her skull. A body sculpted out of marvel. The looked around, neon flashes and burst of dazzling lights reveling a Greek pantheon of Gods and Goddess.

"The benefits of having that pesky Y chromosome. Better metabolism, less muscular loss as you age, a good diet makes keeping the baby fat easy as pie, and better BMI ratio."

"Better bodies than," Amanda was at a loss for words.

"Guys," James handing her a cocktail, "have the best female bodies in the world. Plus, trannies are accustomed to plastic surgeries. If God shortchanges them then science and questionable medicine will pick up the ball."

The place, Amanda soon realized, was a bad, tacky and kitsch remake of a 70's disco… in all the good ways. The whole established was barely gripping the edge of decency. The sensible part of her brain told her to get the hell out off Dodge. The part of her brain, that vestigial tail that came into being the second Moira walked into her life, that wayward piece she desperately tried to snuff out under a coat of corporate America, that drunk hillbilly demon that shot up her veins with moonshine and dared her to go up to a cop and flick the law the bird, that part, well, that part was handing her tequila shots and telling her to get into the conga line of strapping young men, under clothed women and Barbie doll shemales. Conga it is, Amanda told her lizard brain.

The night bore on. Shots. Butts. Small talk. Grouping hands. Frisky looks.

"You're going to love this," James taking her up a spiral staircase into another floor. "Just hold tight to my hips and enjoy the ride." Amanda put her arms around James' waist, grabbing his belt. He guided her into a dark corridor. Small, almost imperceptible U.V lights hanging by a line in the ceiling; a miner's shaft. It was an urban cave

"What the hell is that?"

"The Tunnel of love," James took her in.

"Holy shit," out the other end they came 5 minutes later. "It's like the boat ride from Willy Wonka. Weird, psychedelic and a bit scary."

"Also sexy as hell," James said. "Manage to see anything. It's tricky with the lights."

"A live sex show," Amanda recapped. Inside the tunnel, a mass of flesh. Dozens of people were participating in an open orgy.

The next few hours went by in a dreamy haze. Amanda went to the bathroom only to be offered blow and X. "Maybe next time." She skated up to the bar and found herself doing a Beyonce number with three other girls… or at least she though they were girls… on top of the counter. "Jesus, where the hell did they learn to move like that?" The place was packed and no-one gave a fuck what the other thought. It was freedom from all restriction.

"In here," a handsome Brazilian transvestite told her, "everything is permitted, as long you're not bothering anybody. You're hangups, your extra luggage and quirks, become a problem the second you start stockpiling them on someone else's front porch."

The night rattled off with the ferocity of a Tommy Gun; short burst of wild gunfire, *ratatatatata* flashes, punctuated with moments of inactivity. 10 minutes of dazzling out of this world encounters with charming strangers, coupled with 20 minutes of dullness. It slugged on. James always by her side. The guy couldn't keep his hands off her. He was strutting around the place, shouting names, fetching drinks, telling her tall tales of his exploits.

"You really don't have to try to impress me," she said. "I like you already." To prove her point, Amanda took James back into the tunnel of love. Inside she kneeled, unzipped his fly and gave her date a blowjob. He came in her mouth, she swallowed every drop.

They were about to go home, when the handsome Brazilian came up to them and asked: "you two up for a party?"

Amanda retorted, "what sort of party?" That question, by some loophole in the fabric of space and time, some physic's disapproved glitch, lighspeeded her back to her apartment; naked, sitting cross-legged on the floor, her hands bound against a post of her bed and watching James perform a fellatio on someone else.

If she was hard-pressed, strapped to a lie detector, she would have given an investigative team a point-by-point rehash of how she had ended in that peculiar position. She looked down, James' semen already drying on her pink breast and started ticking of bullet points in her brain. She would have signaled out the fact that the transvestite, Felicitas, had grabbed both of their arms and taken them to another club. She would have pointed out that at that club, Felicitas, bought a pitcher of Sangria. She would have highlighted the fact that the three of them downed the whole thing in less than 20 minutes. Amanda would have place particular emphasis on Felicitas' hand going up and down her knee below the table. She would have stressed that the charming, coquettish and drop dead gorgeous tranny - long auburn hair, eyes to die for, and a body that was Sports' Illustrated Swimsuit Issue worthy - had been playing with the back of James' neck. She would have underline the fact Felicitas trying to get into James' pants hadn't brought about an attack of jealousy but a shower of pleasure. Amanda would have drawn attention to her disinhibited behavior, an errand leftover from Moira's programing, had compelled her to act. She bend over the empty pitcher and started to kiss Felicitas; prying a mouth open with her lips and sucking the girl's tongue. Amanda would have given due prominence to James' paying the bill in a hurry, and all three of them - on mass - stumping out the club. And, above all, Amanda would have accentuated, with bold red ink, the speed with which she drove to her apartment, Felicitas giving James a blowjob in the backseat.

"God, I want to fuck both of you," she ran a stop sign and crossed an intersection in red. It had taken them less than 15 minutes to tie her to the bedpost, on Amanda's urging. "Why do you have so much parachord?" James still in dark on the whirlwind that was Moira. Before she could answer, the Brazilian took the lead and squashed James' curiosity. Felicitas, still dressed, continued giving James the backseat blowjob. When James was about to cum, Felicitas pointed him towards Amanda and…That basically explained the sticky mess on her belly.

Now James was completely naked and Felicitas was slowly undressing. Her blouse going over her head. Her pants had been torn off by James; the fabric a massive speedbumb in the guy's plan of attack.

Amanda saw how her boyfriend - I guess she could call James her boyfriend after this - was sticking Felicitas' cock down his throat. The girl's penis was like the rest of her, incredibly feminine; which is sort of like an oxymoron. It was dainty but pointy. It wasn't massive but it managed a powerful erection. It was more like a flute than a baseball bat. It was beautiful. And the way Felicitas pounded Jame's mouth proved that what she lacked in girth, she made up in experience and tactics.

James was really going at it, he was in a thug of war battle; Felictas would pull out and he'd hungrily dive for the retreating cock. He had never before been with a transvestite. It was an item on his bucket list that he could know scratch off. The first thing, at least with Felicitas, that he noticed was the fact that Trannies didn't test the waters. They didn't dip their toes into a new sexual partner's swimming; they dive-bombed and belly flopped into the deep end. Felicitas hadn't needed much encouragement, she was game for everything. James was a bit taken aback by his boss' brazen attitude. Amanda, his girlfriend? - he'd table that for now - was a wildcat with a mean streak and a potent libido that really took no prisoners. Felicitas pulled his hair and went all the way in. He could feel her dick in the back of his throat. He held unto her, extremely well shaped ass, and let her throat fuck him. Amanda, he managed to see, was struggling against the binds; his boss wasn't just turned on, she was on fire.

"My turn," Amanda demanded.

James felt Felicitas leave his gagging mouth. He fell head first, like a big mouth bass out of water, gasping for air, unto the parquet wood polished floor. Then, without even a how do you do, Felicitas started drilling Amanda's mouth; a blond head holding for dear life, braced against a wooden pole, getting violently skull fucked. And, you want to know a secret? Amanda not only took it like a champ she gave back. Felicitas started to moan.

The gringa was doing something to her dick. She didn't know what, but the blond could have given every lover she had been with, from Paraguay to Belize, tips on how to give the perfect blowjob. She scraped her shaft with her teeth just enough to cause pain but not anguish. She wrapped her tongue around her meaty downstairs head with expertise; right on the tip, lips enveloped snuggly below the mushroom head. When she went in deep, stabbing Amanda's throat, lips would clamp around her dick's base and a tongue would slither out; sliding its flesh right at the spot where her balls came into being. Amanda's mouth was wet and slippery but not enough that she felt like she was in a slip and slide. And the noises the gringa made; moans with gags, were giving her a hard time. Felicitas was moments away form spewing her juices.

"Why did you stop?" Felicitas said as she stared down. From behind arms wrapped themselves around her body. They pressed har to her chest, she felt James breath on the back of her hair; every follicle standing tall. She felt James' hard erection clash against her behind; the head of his penis, young and pink, running up her crack. She instinctually spread her legs. She was still hard inside Amanda's mouth when James' penetrated her. Felicitas screamed and felt a surge of power batter her insides. She felt James' hot cock forcefully ramming itself into her.

Amanda felt Felicitas cock pulse in her mouth. She unclamped and let it rest for awhile in the pillow of her tongue. Felicitas arms felt to each of her sides. She saw the transvestite grab hold of her bead, claw the sheets and brace herself. She didn't need to see what was happening to know that the night had gone off the deep end in a good way. She felt Felicita's buckle against her. She felt Felicita's body being forced and manhandled. She heard James groan; her boyfriend, her lover, penetrating the girl she was sucking off analy. Amanda wanted to be part of fun.

Her penis was almost spat out. Felicitas looked down and understood why. Amanda had spread her legs, tucked her knees against her waist… an invitation if there ever was one.

James felt as Felicitas started to kneel. He keep thrusting his cock into her. His groin bounced with fury of two cheeks that could have made any man rethink their sexual orientation. He slid down, never disconnecting and realized what was about to happen.

Amanda gasped in pain and exhilaration. In one fluid motion Felicitas had snatched her knees and forced them up. She was still tied up to her waist, so some discomfort was expected. Her pussy open wide free and vacant… Then, while she was till trying to hold tight to the dynamics, the vacancy sign switched off. Felicitas penetrated her and it was incredible. The three were connected. When James pushed, Felicitas pushed, when James pulled out, Felicitas pulled out. Amanda had no control, for that matter Felicitas had also resigned and curbed dominion. The had become subjects to James' dominance; the man overseeing every aspect of their pleasure.

Felicitas felt James cock turn to granite inside her.

Amanda, moaned as Felicitas' erection was ratchet up to eleven; bulging and quaking inside.

James could hold it any longer, he plunged deep and filled Felicitas' ass with his cum. He never let go, he never retreated.

Felicitas started to spasm inside of her and Amanda felt like a God in complete command of her bliss. She wrapped her legs around

Felicitas waist and was rewarded by the fact that her ankles reached James' behind; her boyfriend started to stroke the soles of her feet. Felicitas was catching her breath, when she heard Amanda whisper a demand at James.

James pulled out and said, "yes, sir!"

The gringa was insane Felicitas said as James bend down and started cleaning his girlfriend's snatch, while paying close attention to her moist cock. Yup, they were defiantly two nutballs and quite possibly a great match.

STAYS IN MEXICO

"'You want something illegal?' That was one of the first things we were asked on our trip to Cancun. Out off the airport, into the hotel shuttle, the driver turns and gives us that sale's pitch. That's the thing you have to understand about Mexico, everything has a different dynamic. Mexico is what Las Vegas used to be. Whereas that Nevada goldmine is regulated horseplay. Sin City a responsibility free-zone by way of the Disney Corporation. Everything giving off the illusion of danger and of that power reversal ritual the blue collar mass is desperate for. The spot, in reality, one of the most regulated regions in the United States. It's hookers and gangsters in the same way those plastic palm trees and the guy in the Stitch costume in Magic Kingdom are real; all make believe. Mexico, meanwhile, is the real deal. The Riviera Maya a free-for-all buffet for every gringo to get their jollies off. The cops are in on it. The Narcos are right there in your hotel lobby. Scoring sex is as easy as downloading an app. In other-words, it was the percent place for Joaquin.

I wasn't blind, when I got married to him I knew exactly what I was getting into… and after almost three years of celibacy, what I was getting into was the complete package; at least downstairs. Joaquin was a poon-hound from the day I meet him, until I slipped him his divorce papers. Amanda give me all manner of trash concerning that aspect of my 20 years junior latin husband… Like I didn't know. After her dad, I could spot a cheat a mile away. Unlike her dad, Joaquin still had enough ammo in his gun, after going to the shooting range, to come back home and fuck me silly; not just give me a pat on the back and say 'long day at the office. Going to sleep.' It's not so much that I forgave Joaquin, it was more along the lines that I didn't really give a fuck. He could dip his cock in every pussy in the State as long as he'd come home and give me an orgasm. The thing about Joaquin that really started to grate my nerves was the very thing I found enchanting in the first place. 'Honey, Amanda, don't call him a dumbass, can't you see it's a cultural thing? It's the language barrier, english being his second language. It's the fact that he was raised in Costa Rica. It's his lack of a proper education. But he's smart where is counts.' Well, I can admit when I'm wrong. Joaquin was intellectually bankrupt. He thought ZZ Top was a Yiddish cover band.

My first marriage was a sexual fiasco, but at least Amanda's dad could carry a decent conversation. Joaquin couldn't keep the narrative of Saturday morning cartoon straight in his head. He wasn't a bad guy per say, he was just a young guy - one who skated on his looks - with little to no ambitions. But, dear God, could he fuck. Once, Demi Moore said, while dating Ashton Kutcher, 'The advantages of a young lover isn't how long he lasts… but how many times he can do it.' Joaquin could rebound in a jiffy; his sexual appetite and his erection on a trampoline. I'd come home, knowing he had been fucking around, only to find him jacking off in the bedroom. Then, while I was still in my work's clothes, he'd pull my panties down and do me against the dresser. At times, he'd do me in the morning, after work, while I was taking a shower and just before falling asleep. He couldn't string two words into a coherent thought, but he could fuck as if it was an Olympic Sport and his multi-million dollar sponsorships was on the line.

First two years, and a good dick and a care-free attitude was enough. By the end of the third, my libido needed a break, and my mind needed some stimuli. I knew that the marriage was on the fritz. It was simple arithmetic. Sex, at most, on a good day, only amount to, combined, about 1 hour. That left about 5 hours of actual couple's time to get through. The math didn't add up. And on weekends, when it was just the two off us, our kids out on the town and our work on standby, time slugged by with the haste of a turtle with cement boots.

'Hey, you want to go to Cancun?' He went one sleepy afternoon, nothing more to binge watch on Netflix.

A week later we landed in Mexico and went to an all inclusive. At night, I'd stay by the Landshark Bar - having a blast singing Karaoke with a gaggle of Ex-Pats - while Joaquin went out on the boardwalk. He'd come back, 'went to Coco-Bongo', smelling of cheap booze, cheaper weed and dime-store pussy. Then, he'd fuck me silly; in other words, the regular shit.

One day, while my hubby was away, I got to talking to a High School teacher from Minnesota. Fella' my age. Balding and graying. A paunch of a good life and affluence hanging by his waist band. I wouldn't have given him a second look, not with the beefcake I had in my room, if it wasn't for the awesome Hawaiian Shirt he was sporting.

'Is that Mickey fighting a crocodile?'

'Damn straight,' he downed a Corona. 'Bought it at the Magic Kingdom, just outside the Jungle Cruise. Names, Pete.'

Turns out he was on a family vacation. His sister had just beaten breast cancer and the clan decided to celebrate by going to Cancun. His wife had passed away from a stroke 5 years before.

He was charming. He was social. He was an academic. And, more importantly, he could name the 4 Beatles without missing a beat. He was everything Joaquin wasn't.

Then, Pete invited me to get a gander of his mini-fridge; an exact duplicate of the one I had in my room, Pete was anything but subtle. I understood the innuendo… he might as well have asked me if I wanted a nightcap or to come up for a coffee.

To say I was tipsy would have been the understatement if not the year, the freaking century. But, I wasn't loopy or hazy on account of the Mexican hooch, I was tripping on something I had known I was desperately in need of; a tall class of mature companionship. Joaquin was Jose Cuervo Tequila, while Pete had the rough attitude and the homegrown personalty of great Bourbon. He had been aged, wriggles and all, by life. He was bittersweet, cutting to swallow, but with a smooth finish.

I started making out with him as soon as I entered his room. Then, mid grouping session, the door flung open and in walks another man. The spitting image of Pete, only younger and with a couple of pounds missing in the abdomen. Josh was Pete's little brother, they were sharing the room and scaling back costs.

'For a college professor,' I remember telling him, 'you really need to get a handle on the whole tie on the doorknob bit.'

Josh was about to do a Roadrunner skip out the door, when, I went and offered him a cerveza. I put a kibosh on Pete's grand plan. We started sharing war stories. Josh, it seemed worked as a graphic designer in San Diego. The family had been estranged and it had taken one of them getting a death sentence to pull them back into a unit. The Cancun trip was as much a celebration of their sister kicking cancer in the ass, as well as a blood reunion of grade A personalities. They were getting to know each other once again. Pete kept undressing me with his eyes, while his brother prattled on and on about operating systems and technical jargon. His intense focus was making me wet. I looked at my watch and realized that the midnight hour was approaching; I had at most four hours before Joaquin stumbled back into my life. I went and took a chance. When in Mexico, right?

'So,' I got up and addressed the siblings, 'when are either of you going to round up your cojones and finally fuck me?' They looked at me like I had just grown another head… but they did not flinch. I already had my sandals off, so slipping out of my sundress turned out to be a synch. I wasn't counting on hooking up with two complete strangers, so I made it a point to also scrape off my Hane's cotton undergarments - what Amanda called my granny pants - with the frilly Caribbean dress. I stood naked in front of them, going for broke, putting it all on the line. Waiting for one of them, any of them, to act.

Then, before shame slipped under the doorway, both of them reacted. They stumbled on each other. Pete pushed Josh out of the way, reached me and started to bite my neck with the passion of parched man having come out of the Sahara straight into a water fountain. He drank me in. Josh meanwhile took his clothes off and came at me from behind. I still remember his member already hard, digging at my backside, his hands cupping my breast, his lips and tongue tracing a small line down my spinal column.

Pete went down, past my belly button, kissing his way down my chest and belly, until he reached the top of my pelvis. He lingered there, nipping with small bites. I placed my hands over his head, as Pete parted my legs and started, in that awkward position to eat me out.

Josh, started to play with my ass. I let go of Pete's head, and reached for Josh's cock. I started to stroke it. When I was wet, incredibly wet, and well lubricated by Pete, Josh threw me against the bed and penetrated me in the classic missionary position. He went all the way in. Soft at first, letting my pussy adjust to his tool, and then fast. Pete started to play with my tits, while he took off his clothes. No sooner were his pants out that I had him inside my mouth.

Josh, kept at it for 10 minutes and then I felt him cum inside of me. He moaned and got incredibly hard before exploding. I shuttered. He withdraw and Pete, already on the verge of climaxing, flipped me over, hung my knees on the edge of the bed, and came at me. He penetrated my pussy. I felt his penis mingle with his brother's cum. He held my knees apart, and took his sweet time drilling me. He couldn't stop complementing my ass. I reached down and played with my clit, my fingers feeling the hardened flesh of his erection. For a man past his prime, Pete knew how to last. 20 minutes in, sweat dripping onto my back, Josh once more hard and waiting for his turn, Pete finally finished… and, for the first time that night, so did I.

I wanted to get up, I wanted to take a shower, I wanted to, perhaps get a grip on reality and commonsense, Josh dashed those hopes against a rock. He pushed me to one side, spread my legs and hooked one against his shoulder, then, while I was adjusting to the new position, he once more penetrated me.

They took turns on me. I must have had about half a dozen orgasms before the night was over. They fucked me on the bed. They fucked me on the coach. They fucked me in the veranda that over looked the swimming pool. They fucked me in the shower. Pete ate me out while Josh held my arms and immobilized me. I gave Josh a fantastic blowjob, while Pete pushed my head against his brother's cock; he held me tight, forcing me to deep-throat his sibling when Josh started to cum. I swallowed Josh's load and let Pete, the ass fan that he was, finish on my but cheeks.

I went back to, what I already knew was a failed marriage, bowlegged and raw. I made Joaquin give me a toque lashing that night; I imagined him tasting something off about his wife's pussy… It was a small conciliation, petty at that, for all the whoring he had done.

For the next two days, Joaquin went to every night club in Cancun, something I encouraged, while I went to Josh and Pete's room. What I discovered, aside from the fact that I was multi-orgasmic, was that it wasn't the sex that drew me back, but the company. Pete would take me out to dinner, before he and his brother defiled me… and in that hour, down by the bar, sharing nachos and tortillas, I realized that he was the sort of guy I could grow old with. That epiphany and the fact that I promised to cash in my miles and visit him in Minnesota were the nails on the coffin of my stillbirth marriage…"

Rebecca.

THE BIG PAYBACK

Andy had just finished, he lay exhausted on Amanda's naked body. The sight that had thrown him over the edge was that of his wife Penny giving her coworker a sixty-nine while said coworker was being penetrated.

That night with Nick had been worth every hair-raising and questionable action… Plus, to be fair, it had been a blast. Sex, above everything else, had to be fun.

Penny flopped onto the side and demanded that Andy finger fuck her while Amanda answered a call; her cellphone had been going insane, the rings mixing with her moans, for the last half hour.

Andy started to penetrate Penny with his ring finger and then his middle, she twisted her nipples and pinched them. Penny's eyes ping-ponged between Andy's body, his dick slowly but surely rising once more, and Amanda's naked form on the cellphone.

"Guys," Amanda told them, hand over the phone's mic' "you really want to have some fun?"

Penny gave off a small shrill that both meant she was in the zone as well as: "what did you have in mind?"

"My boyfriend, James, wants to come over… He's a really open-minded."

Penny and Andy were about to say, "hell yes", when the night decided to get wacky on all of them. Like something ethereal and supernatural, a voice said from one corner.

"I'm I invited?"

The three of them turned.

"Shit!" Amanda shouted. "How the hell did you get in here?"

"I can pick a lock," Moira said.

… To be continued.

Lightning Source UK Ltd.
Milton Keynes UK
UKHW010611220922
409256UK00001B/43